THE PRISONER

THE MESSES SERIES, BOOK FOUR

KIERSTEN MODGLIN

Cover Design by Kiersten Modglin
Copy Editing by Three Owls Editing
Formatting by Kiersten Modglin

First Print and Electronic Edition: 2018
kierstenmodglinauthor.com

To my fans.
To the ones who begged for more after reading Gunner's story.
It's entirely because of your love for these characters that this Mess-y world exists.
Thank you for following me on this amazing journey.
I hope you've enjoyed the ride.

A LETTER TO MY READERS

Dear Reader,

This is the fourth, and final, installment in The Messes Series. While the other books in this series don't necessarily have to be read in order, **this book must be read last.** This story will feature several familiar faces and the ending to some storylines that were previously left open. If you haven't read books one, two, and three, it's super important that you do that first before reading any further.

Here are the other titles, in order, so that you may find them easily:

The Cleaner (The Messes, #1)
The Healer (The Messes, #2)
The Liar (The Messes, #3)

. . .

ONCE YOU'VE READ THEM, come back here and finish out this amazing series. I hope you will enjoy it!

XO,

Kiersten Modglin

PS: WATCH FOR SOME "EASTER EGGS" throughout the book—there are four! I'd love to hear if you catch them!

ONE

FIONA

They believed she was a monster. And, she guessed, maybe she was. All she knew was that she'd done what she had to do. To survive. To protect herself. To protect them.

Fiona Denali drove the bustling interstate with a vacant mind. The radio in her beat up car didn't work, but that was okay. She liked silence. Preferred it, in fact. It left her mind free to wander. The gas light on the dash lit up and she frowned, searching for the next exit sign. She'd just crossed over into Tennessee, a state she'd briefly called home at one point, hoping to get lost in a busier city than the one she'd left.

As the exit ramp approached, she switched lanes, pressing her brake slightly. She let out a sigh as she saw the gas prices. The money she'd made in the last city was dwindling. She'd have to stop soon in order to make some more.

Settle down for a bit, but never for long. That was her rule. She had to keep moving, keep pressing on.

She pulled into the gas station, parked next to a pump, and climbed out of the car. She took a deep breath, stretching her arms above her head. When she walked into the building, she pulled out the tiny black wallet she carried, laying a one hundred dollar bill on the counter. The attendant stared at her. "We can't take that," he said.

"What do you mean you can't take it?" she asked, already irritated with his whiny voice and cystic acne.

He pointed to a blue sign beside the register that read, **Attendant Accepts Bills $20 and Under.**

She groaned. "I don't have anything else."

"I'm sorry," he said, clearly not sorry. "It's policy."

"What kind of shit policy is that? I need gas and I have cash. Why the hell can't you take my hundred? Hold it up to the light or whatever. It's fine," she said, shoving the bill closer to him.

He pushed it back. "I'm sorry," he repeated. "You'll have to come back with something smaller."

"I don't have anything smaller. And I need gas now. You're the only station at this exit."

He shrugged. "I need you to step aside, so I can help the next customer."

"Are you serious right now? You're turning away a paying customer."

His face remained expressionless. "I don't make the rules, lady. Next," he called, looking to the man standing behind her.

She snatched the money from the counter, muttering under her breath and storming out of the building, boiling with rage. She walked to her car, staring around. It was no use. There hadn't been another station on the sign and she could see for miles on the flat stretch of highway. She groaned, climbing into her car and placing her head on the steering wheel. She tried to think, quickly, of what she could do. There was nowhere around to break her bill. She could try and get a random customer to give her the change, but what were the chances of that? She certainly wouldn't do it if the situation were reversed. Knowing her luck, the person would end up running off with her money.

A knock on her window caused her to jump. She lifted her head, looking over. There was a man standing outside of her car. He wore a flannel shirt and a beanie on his head; curly, chin-length brown hair framed his face. She leaned over, turning the window crank so it would lower just a bit. "Yeah?" she asked.

"Hi," he said sheepishly. "Sorry if I startled you. I heard your, erm, encounter with the attendant. I wanted to see if I could help."

"Really?" she asked, feeling skeptical. "Why?"

"You looked like you could use it," he said, shrugging.

"Thank you." She nodded. "If you could just break this hundred, you'd really be doing me a favor." She held out the bill.

"Actually, I wanted to see if you could do me one in return," he said, his breath fogging up the crisp fall air.

Her heart sank, knowing it couldn't have been that easy. "What do you want?" she asked, eyeing him. She hadn't always been above doing *anything* for cash, but she'd made a vow to herself that she'd be better than that. Or at least try. She had to find her morals again. Whatever they may be.

"I need to get away from here," he told her. "I'll pay for your gas in exchange for you taking me with you."

"Taking you with me? You have no idea where I'm headed."

"I'm not headed anywhere specific," he said. "Wherever you can take me. However far you want. I have money, and I'll keep your tank full as long as you're willing to have me tag along."

"Why?" she asked.

"Just looking for a change of scenery," he said. She knew he was lying but, honestly, what choice did she have? It was a hard offer to pass up.

"Okay," she said finally.

"Yeah?" he asked, seeming shocked.

She nodded. "Go fill me up."

"Uh, you have to come with me," he told her.

"Why should I?" she asked, looking around to check and see if someone was waiting for her to step out of the car so they could steal it. She was paranoid, she knew, but life had made her that way and it kept her safe.

"Because I'm not going to go pay for your gas and let you drive away with it and leave me here."

She shook her head. She hadn't thought of doing that. Why hadn't she thought of doing that? "I'm not going to steal from you," she said.

"How would I know that?"

"How do I know you aren't a serial killer?"

"Fair enough," he said, nodding his head. "Tell you what, I'll trust you if you'll trust me."

"Sounds like a fair trade," she said, not telling him there was no way in hell she was going to trust him.

"Okay," he said, studying her face. "You aren't going to leave me?"

"No," she said, "I'm not going to leave." No need to tell him she was planning to use him for the free gas and kick him to the curb first chance she got. He nodded, walking away but continuing to watch her over his shoulder. She got out of the car, ready to pump the gas once he'd given her the okay.

She didn't like this idea. Traveling with a complete stranger. Time had taught her she couldn't even trust those she was closest to, so this was surely off limits. Still, desperate as she currently was, she didn't have room to be picky. Besides, if nothing else, Fiona was savvy. She could take care of herself. Always had. She was going to make sure this little arrangement worked to her benefit. If anyone was going to be double crossed, it wouldn't be her.

TWO

FIONA

Her passenger's name was Logan. That's literally all she had learned about the mysterious man during their drive. He carried one bag—a tattered black backpack. He had no phone that she'd seen him use. Oh, and he apparently was exhausted.

She switched lanes on the interstate, nudging him. "Hey," she said loudly, causing him to jolt from sleep. "Wake up."

He rubbed his eyes, knocking his beanie from his head as he looked around and lifted up from the seat. "Hm? What?"

"I'm pulling over at the next exit. We need more gas, and then I'm going to the rest area so we can sleep."

"Sleep in the car?" he asked.

"You don't seem to be having any problem with it."

"You could let me drive for a bit so you could get some rest."

"Like hell," she said adamantly. "You are not driving my car."

"Fine. It was just a suggestion. Why don't we just stay somewhere?" he asked.

She lowered her brow. "I don't know if you're rolling in money, but I am not. I stay at rest stops all the time. It'll be fine."

Logan shook his head. "I'll pay. Just take us to a hotel."

"You'll pay? What are you? Some sort of eccentric billionaire?"

He didn't meet her eye when he answered. "No," he said finally. "Not an eccentric billionaire. Just a guy who'd like a little privacy for the night."

"Well, that's awfully demanding for someone who's hitching a ride."

"We're stopping anyway," Logan said. "What difference does it make whether we are in a hotel or a rest area?"

She groaned. "You're paying for both of our rooms? I'm not bunking with you."

"Trust me, that was *not* the plan. I will gladly pay for two separate rooms. Hell, I'll pay for two separate hotels. Just get me somewhere I can lay down."

"Oh, yes, you must be *so* exhausted," she said, turning off onto the exit. There was a motel directly across from the gas station, and she pulled into the parking lot after he filled her tank.

"We are not staying here," he said. "Go on down the road and see if you can find something...I don't know, *safer*."

"Pardon me, Your Majesty," she sassed him, "but are you fucking kidding me? It's a place to stay. This one will do fine."

"No," he said, shaking his head. "We are not staying here. Look, just drive a little further. I can afford a nice hotel."

She raised her eyebrows, taking in his words. She'd never stayed at a nice hotel. In fact, it was rare she could even afford a motel as nice as the one he was curling his lip at. It was then she realized what an opportunity she had in front of her. This man had money. Money she could use. She smiled at him.

"Okay, sure," she said finally. "Let's see what else we can find." She pulled out of the lot and drove down the road a bit further. She saw the sign for a hotel up ahead, not too fancy, but nice enough.

"Will this work?" she asked as they neared the turn for the parking lot.

He nodded. "Yeah, this will be fine."

She parked the car, shutting it off and staring at him. "Get out," she said, waiting for him to open his door.

"What?" he asked.

"I'm not getting out until you do."

"What do you think I'm going to do? Steal your car?"

"I have no idea what you're going to do, Logan. But, I'm sure as hell not going to give you a chance to show me."

"I'm not going to steal from you, Fiona," he said, placing his hand on the door handle and climbing out. "You're doing me a favor, remember?"

After he was out, she leaned over and locked his door before climbing out of her own. She walked to the back of the car where he was waiting. "What are you doing?" she asked.

"I was going to get your bag for you," he said.

"I don't need you to." She turned the key, opening the trunk and grabbing her small black bag. "I can carry my own bag."

"Fine," he said, walking ahead of her without another word. They walked into the hotel lobby and up to the counter. A man in a purple dress shirt and tie greeted them.

"Hello, how can I help you?"

"We need to book two rooms, please." Logan pulled out his wallet, and Fiona's eyes widened. The brown leather wallet was filled with cash, enough cash to cause her throat to go dry.

"Room rate is one twenty-two a night, per room," the man told him. "And I'll need your ID."

Logan pulled out his license, handing it and 3 one-hundred-dollar bills over. "Here you go."

The man typed something into the computer and handed his ID back. "And, now I'll need a credit card to keep on file."

Logan turned to Fiona. "Do you have a credit card?"

"What? No," she said firmly. "I thought you were paying for this."

"I am," he said. "In cash. I don't use cards."

"Well, I don't either."

The man at the counter frowned. "We won't charge the card. It's just for incidentals."

Logan sighed. "Can I just leave a cash deposit with you instead?"

The man shook his head, seeming like he was going to turn him down, but when Logan laid two more hundreds on the counter, he nodded. "Okay, fine. We can make an exception this time. I'll just have to have you fill out this form."

Logan nodded, filling it out and taking the room keys. He handed one to Fiona. "There you go."

She took it, heading to the elevator across the hall with Logan right behind her.

"Well, he totally thinks we're criminals," Logan said when the elevator doors closed.

Fiona smiled stiffly. "He's probably right."

"What room are you?" he asked.

She looked down at the envelope that held her keycard. "Room six seventeen."

He held his up. "Six fifteen."

She nodded, not knowing what to say. When they reached the sixth floor and the doors opened, Logan stepped back to allow Fiona out first. "Ladies first," he said.

She shook her head, passing through the opening and checking the sign to see which way her room was. She found it quickly. "Goodnight, Logan," she said simply, slipping the key into the slot.

"What time do you plan to leave in the morning?"

"I'm not sure," she said. "Early probably. To get a headstart." A headstart to where, she wasn't sure.

"Okay, I'll set an alarm. Goodnight." With that, he walked into his room and she disappeared into hers.

FIONA STEPPED INTO THE SHOWER, the hot water burning her skin. It had been so long since she'd been able to take a proper shower; washing herself in gas station bathrooms had gotten old quick and though she had some cash saved up, it was never enough to waste on a room to sleep in for a few hours.

The clothes from her bag were in the bathtub with her and she pulled up the plug so they could soak. She squirted the small complimentary bottle of body wash into the tub and let it lather up so her clothes could be washed. Along with her body, she'd been washing her clothes in public sinks and they were starting to smell again. Not that it mattered, really. Not that anyone cared what she looked or smelled like. Her own brother had deserted her in a city she knew nothing about. The other brother wouldn't piss on her if she were on fire.

She let the water run over her scalp, scalding her skin. She didn't care. Couldn't. She couldn't feel it anyway. Most days she didn't feel anything anymore. Darkness. Emptiness. They were both so familiar to her now.

Fletcher had locked her in a home. *A psychiatric care facility.* A place where she was supposed to heal. But, all she'd done was screw her doctor and take a few pills. Okay, a lot of pills. Three times. She'd just wanted it to be over. Done. She'd just wanted to be as dead to the world as she felt. But, then again, she was dead. Right? I mean, technically. Legally. Gia James was gone and Fiona Denali had died years ago, which was the only reason she'd been able to use her identity. Did it really matter, though? The life that she'd fought so hard to save. Most days it didn't feel like it. Most days she'd rather be dead. Or, maybe she was dead. Maybe this miserable existence was her hell. Alone. Numb. Murderous.

She'd once said that after you'd killed the first time, it wasn't so hard to do it again. She'd been wrong. Holly's death—*Holly's murder*—had destroyed her. She didn't feel bad, necessarily. She'd done what she had to do to protect herself and Fletcher. Her brother had been the weak link in their plan all along. After their disappearance, he'd begged to talk to Holly. Begged to connect with Gunner. It was Gia that had to remind him, over and over again, how badly things could go. How much trouble they'd be in if word ever got out about what they'd done. What she'd done. In the end, Gia had held all of the secrets, enough secrets to break even the most sane mind. And Gia's mind had never been sane—she could thank her mother for that. She was the one who had to protect them all, and now she was the one they hated. She'd done what she had to do. Always. No regrets.

THREE

GIA

TWELVE YEARS OLD

"Do you have to go tonight?" Gia asked her older brother. "It's my birthday."

"I know, Gia," Gunner said. "I'm sorry. I promise I'll make it up to you."

"But, why? Why do you have to go?"

"Because every boy in my class is going to Mark's party. We're staying out of town. In a real hotel. I can't just miss it."

"You care more about Mark's party than ours?"

"Gia, you aren't having a party. You know I love you, but I'm going to the party. I'll be back tomorrow and we can celebrate."

Gia hung her head, and Gunner gave her a quick hug. "It'll be okay," he said.

"You always say that," she whispered.

"And it's always true, right?" he asked, trying to get a smile from her.

"Sure," Gia said, closing her eyes. "Have fun at your party." She walked from his room, her head down, knowing what would likely be waiting for her after Gunner left.

Later that day, Gavin and Gia sat in their room. Gia was in her bed, reading a book, while Gavin played with the small guitar their grandparents had gotten him for Christmas several years ago.

They heard her footsteps at the same time and instantly went stiff. You could almost determine her mood by the way she stomped down the hall. The door swung open with force, and their mother stuck her head in the room.

"Why haven't you started dinner yet?" she demanded.

"I, um, I—"

"I, um, I, I, I," her mother mocked her with a fake whiny voice. "Get in there and get it started. Your dad'll be home soon."

Gia lowered her head, standing up from the bed.

"But," Gavin said, "what about pizza?"

"Pizza?" their mother asked.

"For our birthday," he said quietly.

"Your birthday?" Misty looked up, seeming to think. "Oh, right. Okay." She grunted. "Never mind." With that, she turned around and disappeared from the room.

Gia looked at Gavin. "Never mind? What does that mean?"

Gavin shook his head. "I don't know," he said honestly.

"Do I need to go cook?"

He looked at her, worry on his face. "I don't know. I'll go in there with you if you want."

She nodded. "Please." Her brother stood up beside her, his hand on her back, and led her from the room.

"I've got you," he promised, though they both knew it would do no good if Misty decided she was in a mood. They walked into the kitchen, both shaking, and stopped in the doorway.

Gia's jaw dropped. On their small kitchen table was an open pizza box and a round cake. Misty stood beside the table, a smile on her face.

"Happy birthday," she told them, a twinkle in her eye.

"Mom?" Gavin asked. Gia was utterly speechless, relief flooding through her.

"You didn't think I really forgot your birthdays, did you?" she asked, her hands on her hips. "Thirty-seven hours in labor, you don't forget that."

Gia tried to smile, though she still felt uneasy. "Thank you, Momma."

She smiled. "Sit down and eat," she told them, handing them each a paper plate. "Before it gets cold."

They did as they were told, pulling out the wooden chairs and taking a seat. It was so rare they saw their mother in a good mood, Gia couldn't help but wonder when the storm behind her wild eyes was going to make landfall.

She took a piece of pizza from the box carefully, setting it on her plate and waiting. Gavin went next, taking his piece and setting it down. Finally, their mother grabbed one. Gia picked at the cheese around the edges of the crust, waiting for a signal that it was okay to eat. She never knew what it was that would set her mother off.

Just then, the front door opened and they heard their father's footsteps as he walked through the quiet house.

"Come eat dinner," Misty called to him before he'd made it into the kitchen. Within seconds, he appeared, covered in grease. His latest job was at a local mechanic shop, but it didn't really matter. They never lasted long. Between his alcoholism and general bad attitude, he never seemed to make it past a month or two before he'd be let go.

He smiled at them, his eyes red and bloodshot. "Happy birthday," he said, his words already slurring. He'd been drinking on his way home. It wasn't unusual. Her father's favorite hobby was to pick up whole pints of whiskey and drink them on his drive across town.

"Thanks, Dad," Gia said softly as her father slammed down in the seat next to her. He smelled of gasoline and cheap whiskey, a smell that made her stomach turn instantly.

He patted her shoulder, his grip sloppy, before slipping a slice of pizza from the box and taking a bite. "Delicious," he said, giving her a wink.

She tried to smile at him, but her mother's menacing glare caused her to look away.

"How was work?" Misty asked, sliding her hand across the table to grip Rick's.

"Work was fine," he told her.

"Did you miss me?"

"Always," he said without looking her way.

Misty moved her hand away. "Did you pick up the kids' gifts?"

"Gifts?" he asked. "Was I supposed to?"

She groaned, rubbing her forehead. "No, I guess not. I should've sent them to pick out their own gifts, huh?"

Rick shook his head. "You didn't say anything about it, Misty. Do you want me to go get them something?"

"It's fine," Gavin said plainly. Gia grimaced. They'd never gotten gifts on their birthday. Not for as long as she could remember. This was clearly just Misty trying to start a fight.

"No, it's not," Misty said. "I wanted to get you both something special."

"I'll go back to town and get—"

"I said no," Misty screeched. "It's too late now. The surprise has been ruined."

"Misty, for god's sake, I didn't—"

Misty stood up from the table dramatically. "Just forget it," she cried, storming out of the room.

Rick looked to Gia, a pitiful look on his face. "I'm sorry, kiddo. I'll pick you both up something tomorrow."

"Don't worry about it, Dad. It's not a big deal," Gavin answered. "We weren't expecting anything."

Rick patted both their heads. "Where's your brother, anyway?"

"He went to Mark Davis' birthday thing," Gavin said. "It's an overnight party."

Their father nodded his head slowly. "He's missing out on cake, then," he said, reaching to open the plastic around the cake. Before he could pull it off, Misty sighed dramatically from the living room, fake sobs echoing through the house. Gia bit down on her tongue, knowing what would be coming. "I guess I'd better go check on her," Rick said, sliding the cake toward Gia. "Go ahead and slice it." He kissed their heads. "I'll be right back."

As he walked out of the room, Gia took a bite of her pizza, her belly beginning to grumble. Gavin also began scarfing his down with ravenous hunger. He grabbed a second piece before the first was even gone. Gia was slower. Even though she'd always been relatively thin, she wasn't naïve enough to not notice the fact that her jeans had gotten a bit tighter than normal lately.

She chewed the last bit of pizza, dusting her hands on her pants. "Should we cut the cake?" she asked.

"I don't know," Gavin said, his mouth full. They never knew what their mother's trigger would be that night. Especially with the mood she was already in. If they didn't cut the cake, she could be mad that she'd wasted her money on ungrateful kids. If they did, she could be mad that they'd thought only of themselves when she was obviously upset. If they went to check on her, she could be mad because they weren't minding their own business. If they didn't, they would be called selfish brats. It was a balancing act. Every day. Knowing when to toe the line. Trying to read her every mood. It never got easy, and they never got better at it. They had the scars to prove it.

LATER THAT NIGHT, *after the latest argument between her parents had calmed down, Gia crept from her bedroom toward the kitchen. She flinched upon seeing her mother standing at the counter, but she'd already been seen.*

"What are you doing up?" Misty asked, her voice harsh.

Gia clenched her fists by her sides, trying to make herself feel braver than she did. "I just wanted to get some water."

"Hmph," her mother hummed.

Gia walked past her toward the sink, grabbing a glass from the cabinet and filling it from the tap. She gulped the water down quickly, just wanting to make it back to her bedroom. Just wanting to get somewhere safe. Safer. She was never truly safe with this woman.

She washed the cup out with soap quickly, not wanting to do anything that might set her mother off, and set it in the drainer. She hurried past her, holding her breath.

"Wait," Misty said. "Take this to your father." Gia turned around. Her mother was scraping the last of the crushed up white pills into her father's tumbler. She stirred it with her finger until the powder had dissolved, licking the drink from her finger and handing the cup to Gia.

Gia took it with shaking hands. If her mother was planning on knocking her father out, she knew the night would be bad. They never knew what would set nights like this in motion—honestly most of the time, it was absolutely nothing—but they'd learned at a young age what it meant when Misty crushed up the pills for his drink. In an hour, he would be knocked out cold. And then, she would come for them.

FOUR

FIONA

Fiona was sitting at the end of the hotel bed, chewing nervously on her fingernails. She looked at the door again. She knew what she had to do. She'd known it from the second she'd seen the cash in his wallet. Eventually, his generosity and need for a ride would run out, and she'd be left alone. And with a dwindling cash supply, she'd be forced to resort to finding new ways to bring in cash. Ways that didn't involve a 401(k) or health insurance. The things she'd had to do for money, the things she'd had to do to survive, made her shudder. She shook her head. It wasn't a choice. None of it was a choice. In the end, it always came down to her or them. And it would always be her.

Except for killing Danielle. That was for Fletcher. Her penitence for all she'd done to hurt him. She was sorry. Sorry she'd left him alone, though it had been his choice to leave her in that clinic. Sorry she'd taken Holly and his child away.

But she wasn't sorry for saving his life. She wasn't sorry for protecting him at all costs, even when that meant protecting him from himself.

Fletcher would never see that, though. The brother that she'd lived for, the brother she would've died for...he'd never trust her again. Not that she could blame him, she guessed. He didn't see the danger that Holly's pregnancy had put them in. But, nonetheless, his abandonment stung.

Deep down, Fiona had always believed it would be her and Fletcher until the end. They'd spent every moment of their lives together, practically. Until she'd had to make a choice—their lives or their friendship. And she'd chosen their lives. She'd saved them. She'd do it again in a heartbeat.

That was why she'd chosen to save the girl Fletcher seemed to love. Because he deserved someone. Someone he could be with until the end, even if Fiona had to be alone. The doctor, Neville, that she'd been sleeping with at the clinic, the one with the rotten milk breath and beady eyes, had given her Fletcher's address the night she left. The night he snuck her out. She'd made sure to have him change Fletcher's number in the computer. She didn't want him to be called. She didn't want him looking for her. But, still, she wanted to make sure he was safe. For a few nights, she'd slept with strange men, picking up several hundreds here and there to get her by. When she had enough, she'd bought a car. A cheap clunker with more miles than a school bus and smellier than one, too. Then, she'd planned to check on Fletcher. Once she saw that he was safe—happy—she'd be on her way. She couldn't face him again. When she'd seen him, it had been early morning. He'd run right past her, heading to an apartment building a few blocks away. She'd waited, watching the building for hours.

When he'd finally left, he'd been with a man who had coal black hair and tremendous fashion sense. She followed them, wanting to catch a glimpse of what Fletcher's life looked like now, though they went much further than she'd planned to go. She'd followed them to Dakota, surprised to see he'd go so close to the town they'd once called home. And that's when she'd seen her. She parked a block away, hiding behind the dumpster at a nearby abandoned building, and watched. When she'd seen the girl, the cop, approaching the house, she'd been ready to act. She wasn't going to let her brother take the fall for all she'd done. It had always been her or them, but for her brother, there was no contest. If she had to choose between her or him, she'd choose him every time. Even if he didn't see it that way.

The cop was called into the house, and an hour later when Gunner had showed up, Fiona knew it couldn't be good. Had they killed her? But then, there she was. And Fletcher's arms were around her as they crossed the street, headed for the small white house. Fiona watched as he kissed her forehead, a look in his eyes Fiona hadn't seen him have for anyone but Holly. Before Holly, it had always been her. Until now. It stung, knowing she'd been replaced. Fletcher had someone new in his life, someone who hadn't hurt him like she had. Someone who could be the person he needed. She should've left then. She didn't belong there anymore. And yet, she stayed. She stayed, watching her brothers with their new lives. All of it without the sister who'd ruined everything. They were better off without her. Everyone was.

So, when she saw the girl come outside with another woman, she'd followed them. She wanted to know more about the woman who could make her brother happy. She wanted to know if she was deserving of his love. She watched them talk, and then watched the woman attack the one Fletcher loved. She hit her in the head with a shovel, burying her quickly. Fiona weighed her options, knowing she had only one. Again, she would kill for the man she wanted to protect.

Even now, she could still feel the knife in her hand, remember the way the cool steel felt as it serrated her skin and clothes. Someone had been coming out the door, and she hadn't had a chance to pull the girl from the grave. She grabbed the body, rushing through the dark bushes and out of sight, hoping and praying her brother would find the girl in time.

She blinked rapidly, pulling herself back to the present. It didn't matter now. The past was in the past and that's where she would have to leave it. She'd learned that much from therapy. Guilt, anger, sadness...the feelings were useless and she'd had to give them up. Now, she was left with quiet emptiness that was much more favorable.

She stood, walking to the door and accepting her decision. She walked through the elevator's doors when they opened, riding down to the lobby. She sighed with relief when the same man who had checked them in was smiling from behind the counter at her. "Hello," he said politely. "Is everything all right?"

"Yes, erm, no," she said. "My friend locked both of our room keys in his room. I wanted to see if we could get another one."

"Okay, sure," he said. "Just one for his room or one for both?"

"His," she said, shocked at how easy it had been. "Room six fifteen."

He nodded, keying something into the computer and grabbing a card from the stack that sat behind the counter. He swiped it through a machine and handed it over to her. "There you go."

"Thank you."

"Have a good night."

She turned around and walked to the elevator before he could change his mind. The slow ride up was filled with racing adrenaline and a sick feeling in her belly. She wanted to do better, be better. She really did. She didn't want to hurt people anymore. But, when she made the decision to break out of the clinic, she also made the decision to survive. She was going to survive no matter the cost. And at this moment, that meant hurting Logan—a man she barely knew. A man she shouldn't care about. So, why did she feel guilty? Why should she feel bad about screwing over a man who, for all she knew, would do the same if the situation were reversed?

She approached his door, keycard in her hand, and took a deep breath as she plunged it into the slot. She turned the handle quietly, peering into the dark room.

Her thin frame fit nicely through the small crack she gave herself to enter, not allowing too much light to creep in. She shut the door behind her carefully, easing the handle up so it didn't 'click' too loudly. She walked down the short entranceway, past the bathroom, and to the bed. A light blanket of moonlight coated the room, illuminating it enough that she could see. He was lying in bed, his back to her.

She hurried to the small desk where his wallet lay, picking it up and opening the pocket. She gasped. It was empty.

"Really?" She heard his voice behind her. She looked over at the bed where he was looking her way. He sat up. "What happened to our pact?"

She laid the wallet down, her face warming from embarrassment. "I need the money," she said simply. As if that justified it.

"Fiona, I offered to pay for your gas. I told you I'll help you."

"You're not helping me. You're helping yourself. You just need the ride. And when you get wherever you're going, you'll walk away and I'll be left to figure out what to do again."

"You don't seem to have any problems taking care of yourself."

"I don't," she said quickly. "But, cash helps. It's nothing personal, Logan. I just needed the money."

He nodded. "How much do you need?"

"You're just going to give me money?" She raised an eyebrow.

"You said you need it, right? Obviously I can't trust you, so I'll give you enough to get you by and let you leave me here."

"Why?" she asked. "Why would you help me at all?"

He was quiet for a moment, then leaned over and flipped on the lamp beside his bed. "Because you seem like you could use it."

"But, I tried to steal from you."

"I know. You don't have to steal. I'll just give it to you."

"I don't understand."

"I have plenty of money, Fiona," he told her plainly. "More than I could ever hope to spend. Giving you the cash in my wallet isn't going to hurt me."

"Fine," she said, holding out her hand. "Then why hide it?"

"I wanted to see what you'd do. I hoped I'd be wrong about you, but I didn't assume I would be."

"How'd you know you wouldn't be asleep when I came in?"

He bit his lip, running a hand through his curly brown hair. "I don't sleep well at night."

"What do you mean you don't sleep?"

"I just...don't."

“You literally slept the whole way here.”

“Nighttime is different.”

“How?”

“It just is, Fiona,” he said, his voice hinting at his frustration.

She swallowed. When was the last time she slept? Really, really slept? It had been so long she couldn't remember.

"Are you okay?" he asked.

She nodded. "Always."

He stuck his hand into the pillow case beside him, pulling out the thick wad of bills. "Here."

She blinked, taking a step toward him. "You're really just going to give it to me? No catch?"

"What catch would there be?" he asked, cocking his head to the side.

She frowned. "I'm not going to sleep with you."

He let out a loud laugh. "Good god, Fiona. I'm not...I didn't...I would never expect that from you." His expression softened as he stared at her. "Have you had sex for money before?"

She crossed her arms. "Well, that's none of your business."

He sat up further, holding out the money. "You're right. It's not."

She took it from his hand, eyeing the cash. It was more money than she'd ever seen before. Enough to keep her going for a while. She offered him a small smile. "Thank you."

"You're welcome. I hope it helps."

She nodded, making her way toward the door. As her hand connected with the handle, she stopped, squeezing her eyes shut. She needed to keep moving, keep walking. And yet, she couldn't. Why? She didn't care about Logan. He was a sucker for handing over his cash to a stranger. So, why did she care what happened to him?

She turned around. "What will you do?" He was still in the same spot, his blue eyes staring at her as she rounded the corner so she could see him again. He had pulled the covers away from his chest, revealing a thin gray t-shirt. When he saw her, he smiled.

"Are you worried about me?" he asked.

She shook her head. "No."

"Are you sure?"

She bit her lip. "I don't care what happens to you."

"Then, why are you asking what I'll do?"

"I don't know." She shrugged one shoulder. "Forget it." She started to walk away again, but his voice stopped her.

"You don't have to be bad, you know."

She spun around. "What?"

"You don't have to be the bad guy, Fiona. You can do the right thing here."

"The right thing?"

"You are obviously feeling conflicted about taking the money."

"So, the right thing is to give it back?" she asked.

"I don't know what the right thing is," he told her. "Only you know that."

"Thanks, Father Owl. Your wisdom is appreciated."

"I'm just saying," he said. "You can be good if you want. There's no shame in being the good guy after having been bad for so long."

"What would you know?"

"Apparently nothing," he said. "But I do know about being the bad guy. And I know about choices and feeling like you have none."

"You know nothing about me," she spat.

"You're right, I don't. Not yet."

"You're barking up the wrong tree, dude."

"What does that mean?" he asked, running a hand through his mop of hair again.

"It means you'll never know anything about me."

"Says who?"

"Says me," she retorted. "I don't trust you."

"And yet, you're the one trying to steal from me."

"I don't have a choice," she told him through gritted teeth.

"There's always a choice, Fiona. Even when it feels like there isn't."

"You have money. You said it yourself, you have more than you can spend. You have no idea what it's like to scrounge for change just to afford a ninety-nine cent burger. Or wash your clothes in a truck stop sink while people bang on the doors because you've been locked in there too long. You have no idea what it feels like to worry about where your next meal will come from or when it will be. Or where you'll be able to sleep, let alone when."

"You're wrong, Fiona," he said. "You're wrong about all of that. I do have money, that much is true, but that doesn't mean I don't have problems. Besides, right now, I can't spend any of the money I do have, so it's doing me no good. The money you have there, plus what little I've kept aside for myself, that's all I own in the world right now."

"What are you talking about?"

He shook his head. "I can't tell you."

She rolled her eyes.

"There's no way you'd hand over nearly all of your money to me. I'm not buying it."

"I have no use for it," he said. "Not without a car to get me away from here."

"You could buy a car with this," she said, holding up the money. "So, why did you need me?"

"I can't buy a car," he said, shaking his head. "That's why I needed you. I can't have anything that could alert people to where I am."

"Alert people? What people?"

"Just...anyone."

She sat down on the end of the bed, noticing the fear in his eyes for the first time. A fear she knew well. "You're on the run." It wasn't a question, but he nodded anyway.

"From who?"

"I can't say."

She bit her lip. "Why don't you just hop in your private jet and fly out of here, then?"

"The people I'm running from don't care about borders, Fiona. If they get a scent of where I am, they'll find me." He paused. "And besides that, I don't have a private jet."

"Well, what kind of rich person are you?"

He laughed. "Apparently not a very good one."

"Well, I'm not a good criminal," she said, staring at the money in her hand.

"You know, it doesn't have to be either or. We can keep with the plan. I'll take care of you, Fiona. You don't have to steal to survive. Not when you have me."

She pressed her lips together, unable to speak. In her whole life, a stranger had never shown her so much kindness as Logan was showing her now. But, she couldn't trust him. Nice as he may be, at the end of the day, he was a stranger. In her experience, even those closest to her were willing to screw her over. Why should a stranger be any different?

"I don't have you, Logan. That's the thing. We're just...two people who happen to be traveling together. You can't trust me, and I can't trust you."

"That's not true," he said. "I do trust you."

"You shouldn't," she said.

"You haven't left with the money yet."

She looked down where the money rested on the bed. "But, I could."

"But, you haven't," he repeated. "And that's the difference."

"The difference in what?" she asked, her voice low.

He squinted his eyes at her, reaching forward to touch her hand. "In everything."

FIVE

FIONA

The next morning, Fiona woke up in the same room as Logan. He'd given her the bed, choosing to sit in the small chair to her right. She hadn't meant to fall asleep, even though she'd told him she would, but eventually she couldn't resist. She stretched, looking over at him. She shouldn't feel so at ease with him. Shouldn't be comfortable enough to sleep in the same room with him. But, her brain wasn't getting the memo.

He smiled at her. "Morning," he said casually, taking a bite from the bagel on his plate. He pointed to an extra plate at the end of the bed. It was loaded up with more food than she'd had in days. "I didn't know what you liked."

She reached for the plate, trying to pretend she wasn't starving, and took a bite of the muffin. Her nose wrinkled involuntarily. "Blueberry?"

He nodded. "Bad thing?"

She put the muffin down. "Beggars can't be choosers, right?"

He smiled, holding out a new one. "I got the last chocolate chip. Would you prefer it?"

She eyed the muffin, her mouth already watering. "It's okay."

"Honestly, you can have it. I like blueberry, too."

"I've already taken a bite out of it," she said, holding hers up.

"I don't mind," he assured her, swapping the muffins.

She took a greedy bite, letting the chocolate surround her taste buds. She let out a moan of delight. "Oh my god, I've missed chocolate."

He grinned. "Eat as much as you want. There's plenty more in the lobby." She ate hungrily, feeling like a pig but too hungry to care. "How long's it been since you ate?" he asked once she'd slowed down enough to answer.

"A few days," she said, wiping her mouth. "It's fine. I've gone longer."

"But you had money. Why didn't you stop to eat?"

"I have to save the money I have. I can't waste it."

"Waste it on a silly thing like food you mean?"

She nodded. "I eat when I have to."

He shook his head. "What are you running from, Fiona?"

"Who says I'm running?"

"Everything about you says you're running."

She bit the inside of her cheek. "Well, if I was, I wouldn't be a very good criminal if I told you what I was running from, now would I?"

"I think we've already established you aren't a very good

criminal," he said, nodding toward the pile of money on the end table.

"Jury's still out on whether I'm taking that."

He nodded. "Chocolate didn't change your mind?"

"About what? Surviving?"

His face grew grim. "About sticking with me."

"Why should I trust you?"

"I don't know," he said simply. "I don't know why you should, but apparently you do or else you wouldn't have fallen asleep. I could've taken the money and your car and left if I'd wanted to."

"But you didn't." She hadn't even considered that possibility. Why hadn't he left?

"I told you, Fiona. I'll take care of you."

She shook her head. "I don't need taken care of."

"Your eyes tell me something different."

She swallowed, looking down.

"So, I'll ask you again...what are you running from?"

She looked up, her eyes full of sorrow. "Myself."

SIX

GIA
SIXTEEN YEARS OLD

Gia walked through the halls between classes with her chin tucked into her chest. She flipped through the book in her hands, wishing she'd had time to finish her homework during class last week. She turned to the page, half-filled out, and groaned. Great, another F. She shook her head, slamming the book shut, and running straight into someone.

"Oof, ouch, sorry," she said, looking up. Her face grew hot with embarrassment as she stared at Alex Donovan, one of the most popular guys in the grade above her.

"Watch it, would you?" he asked hatefully, staring her up and down. His expression changed as she apologized again. "Hey, you're Gunner's baby sister, right?"

She nodded, her lips pressed together as she tucked a stray piece of hair behind her ears. "Mhm."

He smiled when she looked back up at him. "I'm Alex."

"I...I know who you are," she told him, her voice low.

"You do, do you?"

She nodded, trying to get past him. He stepped into her way. "Wait," he said. "Do you want to get something to eat with me sometime?"

She lowered her brow. "Are you serious?"

"Of course," he told her, placing a hand over his heart.

"Um, okay," she said. "Yeah, sure." It felt as though she were in a dream, god knows she'd dreamed of being with a guy like Alex for so long. But she'd never expected it to happen. She was plain. Not ugly, but never beautiful. Guys didn't look at her. Not the way Alex was looking at her now.

"Nice," he said with a grin. "I'll catch you after class?"

"Okay."

He darted past her and she lowered her head, a smile growing on her blushing face. She couldn't believe what had just happened. Had she had any real friends, she would've rushed to tell them. Instead, she'd wait until after school to tell Gavin. Gunner would never understand. He'd say Alex was a jerk. But Gavin respected her decisions. He believed in the good in people. He saw the good in her, though no one else seemed to. That was how her brothers were—one always on the defensive, a forever pessimist; the other a bright side optimist through and through. She hurried to class, wondering just where she fit in between the two.

THAT DAY AFTER SCHOOL, *Gia walked out to the parking lot. Gunner and Gavin would already be gone. They rarely gave her rides, due to Gunner always being at work and*

Gavin always being with girls. When it had come time for the twins to get cars, her grandparents had gotten them both one, but Misty's had broken down and she'd taken Gia's. So Gia was left to walk. She didn't mind it most of the time; their house wasn't too far, and it's not like she had friends who she'd hang out with if she had a vehicle anyway. But, on days like today, when the rain had begun falling, she especially hated not having a car. Not because she minded walking in the rain so much, but because she was afraid of looking stupid and poor. Like she was. Like her family was.

"Hey." She heard his voice behind her, the roaring of his engine as his truck pulled up next to her. "Want a ride?"

She looked up at the truck, shielding her eyes from the rain. "Sure." She pulled open the door, stepping up onto the chrome bar and climbing to sit next to him.

Alex stared at her. "Where do you live?"

She gave him directions, feeling especially needy. "Thank you for giving me a ride. My car's in the shop." She wasn't sure why she'd lied, other than because she wanted to impress him. Alex Donovan was everything every girl craved. He was handsome, athletic, rich, and popular. Sure, he had a reputation, but so did everyone. She was willing to give him the benefit of the doubt.

He pulled out of the parking lot, driving with one hand on the wheel, the other around her shoulders.

"So, about this date," he said finally, "where would you like to go?"

"It's up to you," she told him.

"Lady's choice."

She shrugged. It wasn't like Dale had many options for food—one bar, a small restaurant, and two gas stations. "How about Bennie's?" she asked, hoping she wouldn't make him feel dumb for her choice.

"Sure. We can go to Bennie's. They have awesome cheese sticks," he told her as he turned down her street.

She let out a small sigh of relief. "Yeah, I love them."

"Cool," he said. "You want to go now? Or this weekend?"

She wanted to go then, god knows she did, but Misty would be furious if she didn't make it home in time to clean the house and start supper. She'd be waiting at the door for her to get started. "How about Saturday?" Gia asked.

"Sure, Saturday works. There's a party at Isaac's house that night. We can go there after."

She nodded as he grew closer to her house. "This is it," she said, pointing to the rundown, white home she suddenly felt so ashamed of.

"So, Saturday?" he asked, turning in his seat to face her. "We on?"

She placed her palm on the door handle, nodding quickly as she saw Misty walk to the door. "Yep. Sounds good. Thank you for the ride."

She climbed out the car in a hurry as he rolled down the window. "I'll pick you up at six," he called. She threw a hand over her shoulder to wave at him as she rushed into her house, knowing no amount of Misty's torture could make this day any less perfect.

SEVEN

FIONA

Back in her room, Fiona took an extra shower before they hit the road. The steam felt good against her sore body. What she was sore from, she never knew. Her body was like that of an old woman, always achy and falling apart. Then again, she'd lived through more than most did in a lifetime, so what could she expect?

She ran a hand over her hair, scrubbing the soap into her scalp with vengeance. She had no idea how long it might be before her next shower, and she wanted to make sure this one lasted as long as possible.

Try as she might to avoid it, her mind kept drifting back to Logan. To what had happened between them. To what *hadn't.* She knew there was more to him than what he was telling her. She knew enough to know that he was in trouble. But what kind of trouble? She should abandon him. With or without his money, he could be a danger to her. She was already in enough trouble without getting herself involved with a criminal. Everything in her screamed that she should run away.

So, why couldn't she? Why couldn't she seem to stop thinking of him? His goofy, crooked grin. His curly brown hair she just wanted to run her hands through. The blue eyes she could get lost in.

She was being ridiculous. She was in no position in her life to be getting lost in anyone's eyes, no matter how blue. She couldn't trust him. Didn't know him. She reminded herself of this over and over, and yet it seemed to be lost in translation from her brain to her heart. No matter how much she wanted to abandon Logan, she also wanted to know him more. Her head had always won out in these battles, so why, suddenly, was it her heart that seemed to have the lead?

Once her hair was completely rinsed, she turned off the faucet and stepped out of the shower, wrapping a white towel around her body and tossing another one around her hair. In the clinic, her roots had been forced to grow back out, leaving the muddy blonde only on the bottom half of her hair. She wanted it gone, sick of looking at the murky color, but also wanted to rid herself of the dark hair that had belonged to Gia.

Who did she want to be? She had no idea, honestly. She didn't feel like Fiona and she never wanted to be Gia again, so she was left with being a shell. An empty space in between the girl she'd been and the woman she'd never become. Sometimes it felt like a joke, that she should have to keep living while not really living at all. Nothing felt real. Every day was like a dream, or horrible nightmare, that she was just coasting through on her way to...what? What exactly did she hope for? What exactly did she want her future to look like? At the clinic, she'd decided she no longer wanted to have a future. She'd made that deliberate decision three separate times.

Yet here she was. Living and not living. Dead but not dead.

A rap on her room's door caused her to jump. She opened the bathroom door, cool air hitting her wet skin, and pressed up against the door to look out the peephole. It was Logan. She cursed under her breath, wishing she was dressed. "What is it?" she called.

"Can, um, can I come in?" He looked confused.

"Um, just a second," she told him, hurrying back to the bathroom. She ran the towel over her hair quickly, scrunching the wavy locks in an attempt to tame them.

He knocked on the door again. "Fiona, please let me in."

She sighed, tightening the towel around her chest and hanging the extra one back up before making her way to the door again. She pulled it open quickly. "What?" she asked.

His jaw dropped, looking her up and down. "Oh."

"Can I help you?"

He shook his head, his eyes traveling back up to her face. "Sorry. Can I come in?"

She stepped back, allowing him to pass through. "What do you want?"

"I didn't realize you were...in the middle of something."

"Yes, Logan, I was showering. What do you want?" she repeated. "I need to get dressed."

He nodded. "Yes, you do." He swallowed, seemingly perplexed by the water on her skin. "I was coming to make sure we were planning on leaving today."

"Well, obviously. You had to come right now?"

"I wanted to check on you," he said.

"Why?"

"You seemed upset when you left earlier."

She bit her lip. "I'm fine, Logan." Why did he care, anyway? Why did he have to look so good while he was caring?

"I didn't mean to upset you. I know it's hard to talk about...you know, everything. I just...I'm a good listener, if you need it."

"I don't."

"Okay," he said, his voice so soft she almost missed it. "Fair enough."

"Do you plan on telling me all of your dark secrets any time soon?"

He shook his head. "I'll show you mine if you show me yours."

"Not a chance," she said, putting a hand up over the edge of the towel. He let out a laugh. "What is your obsession with getting to know me, Logan? We aren't friends."

"I never said we had to be friends." His gaze faltered for a moment, falling to the edge of her towel again.

"Then what are you hoping for?"

"More like a mutual understanding."

"Understanding? Of what?"

"Of...look, I don't want to be your friend. But, if we're traveling together, we need to know the basics about each other. We need to at least care that the other makes it through the day."

"Why?" Fiona asked, feeling uneasy. "I don't have to care about you to let you spend your money on me."

"Why is your first response to shut me out, Fiona? Haven't I proven that I'm not going to hurt you by now?"

She shook her head. "I'm not shutting you out. You were never in to begin with. Besides that, no one could ever prove they weren't going to hurt me. Everyone lies."

"Wow," he said, nodding his head slowly. "Someone really hurt you, didn't they?"

She pressed her lips together. "Live and learn."

"It's not really living if you're so afraid to get hurt again you won't put yourself out there."

"I'm not afraid, Logan. I've learned you can't trust anyone. I'm okay with that. Better, actually. More people should try it."

"The world isn't so dark, you know."

"If you honestly believe that, you know nothing about the world I've seen."

"So, tell me about it, then."

"It's a long story, and frankly, not one I want to talk about. Ever. And certainly, not with you."

He nodded, closing his eyes. "Okay."

She held her hand out, gesturing toward the door. "Now, if that's all you needed...I'd like to get dressed."

"I'm not stopping you," he said, not moving.

"I'd like you to leave, Logan."

"Just waiting on you."

"What?"

"I'm waiting on you to get dressed so we can both leave."

"I'm not getting dressed until you leave."

He sighed. "Well, then, we are at a crossroads, aren't we?"

She shook her head. "Get out, Logan."

"Fine," he said. "But, hurry up. I want to get on the road."

She opened the door, shutting it behind him with as much force as the spring weighted door would allow. She let out a breath she hadn't realized she was holding in, walking back to the bathroom and dropping the towel. She looked over her bare body. Her hip bones stuck out too far, something she'd longed for as a teenager, but that was now a sign of how starving she was most of the time. Her skin was dull and dingy, even after her bath. She walked back to the bed, pulling a small pocket knife from her bag. She looked in the mirror, taking it to her hair, and beginning to saw off where the muddy blonde met the black. The knife was dull, and she had to put a lot of force into her cuts, pulling strands from her scalp as she went. When she was done, a pile of hair lay behind her on the floor. She ran her hands along the now shoulder-length ends of her hair and shrugged. Better than nothing.

Suddenly, the door opened again, and she dove for the covers, wrapping them around her exposed skin. "What the fuck?" she demanded, seeing Logan walk around the corner.

"What are you doing?" he asked, a brow raised as he stared at the hair on the floor. "Playing Barber Shop?"

"Can I help you?"

He nodded, holding out a paper cup. "I brought you a coffee."

"How did you get a key to my room?"

"I told them I'd lost it and needed to get in here. Figured I'd take a page from your book." He gave her a wink.

"This isn't working," she said firmly.

"Well, no, it's not really meant to be worn." He ran a finger over the blanket.

"What happened to the shy guy I met yesterday? He

didn't talk. I liked him." He looked at her, his bright eyes connecting with her dark ones, and she took in a sharp breath. His eye contact burned into her, causing her heart to race as he sat down. "Logan, get up." She tried to pull the cover out from under him.

"I can't help but want to get to know what's behind those gorgeous eyes," he said, brushing a piece of her hair from her face. She blinked, suddenly out of her trance, and pulled away.

"Venom and nightmares. There are places in my mind that would terrify you," she said.

"Try me," he begged.

She shook her head slowly. "I need to get dressed."

"Tell me one thing."

"Tell *me* one thing," she spat back.

"What do you want to know?"

"I want to know why you're traveling alone. What you're running from."

"I'm not traveling alone," he said.

"Well, you were before you ran into me. What makes you want to give your money to a random stranger in order to get a ride? I'm not exactly good company."

"Says who?"

"Society." She shrugged.

"Well, I disagree."

"You're avoiding the question."

"I can't answer it, Fiona," he said. "I'm sorry. That's one thing I can't tell you."

"I don't care, Logan. That's the point. I don't care. I'm using you for your money, because it's what I need. So, if you're willing to let me use you, I guess that's fine. Just don't ask me to tell you about myself when you won't do the same."

He looked away. "Fair enough."

"So, can you move?"

He lifted his leg, letting her pull the blanket out from under him and wrap it around herself as she walked across the room and into the bathroom. She shut the door quickly, throwing her clothes on finally and running her fingers through her hair. She closed her eyes, trying to rid the image of his dream-like stare from her mind. Logan was dangerous. More dangerous than she'd realized. In fact, the longer they were together, the easier it would be for him to hurt her. Physical hurt was something she was used to. She could handle it. She was stronger than anything thrown her way. But, emotional pain had been known to destroy her. Leave her broken. It was why she had shut herself down to feeling anything. It was easier this way. And, for quite some time now, it had worked. So, why was Logan suddenly stirring up emotions she didn't know she could have? Yep, he was dangerous, all right. The kind of danger she couldn't afford.

EIGHT

FIONA

Back on the road, Fiona and Logan rode in silence. Every once in a while, Logan would try to start up a conversation, but Fiona shut him down almost instantly. A radio would've certainly come in handy to keep the talking to a minimum, and for the first time she wished it worked.

She shivered, reaching into the backseat and grabbing the only jacket she owned. She pulled it over her lap, trying desperately to warm up.

"You cold?" he asked.

She nodded, staring straight ahead.

"Why don't you turn the heat on?" he asked.

"It doesn't work," she told him. He reached up anyway, turning the knob to turn on the heat. It came on, cool air blowing onto the windshield. "See?"

He frowned, flipping the knob back and forth from cool

to heat, defrost to feet. "It won't switch from defrost or air conditioning?"

"Nope."

"It's probably an actuator. They go out a lot in these types of cars. I can fix it for you."

"What? You're an eccentric billionaire who made his fortune running an auto shop?"

He smiled. "Not even close, but I do know a few things about cars."

She shook her head. "It's not a big deal."

"What about when you need your car for winter? You're going to freeze."

"Maybe I'll head to Florida for the winter so I don't need heat."

"Is that your plan? Make like a bird and fly south?"

"Who says I have a plan?"

"You're way too smart not to."

She glanced at him, her brow furrowed. "How would you know?"

"I'm very intuitive, Fiona," he told her. He pressed the buttons on the dash, holding them in until the yellow lights flashed. Then, he turned the button to face mode, and Fiona gasped as the cool air began blowing through the vents.

"How did you do that?" she asked.

"I told you, I know a few things about cars. I can fix it if you want. Just pull over at the next car parts store so I can find the part."

"Yeah, okay," she said. "No way in hell are you getting your hands on my car."

He sighed. "You'd rather freeze?"

"I've been colder."

“You really don’t trust anyone, do you?”

“No,” she said simply. “I don’t.”

“I’m sorry, Fiona.”

“What are you sorry for?”

"For whatever happened to you to make you so cynical."

"I'm not cynical. I'm strong."

"Then I'm sorry for whatever happened to you to make you so strong." He lowered his gaze. "No one should be so alone."

"It's safer this way," she told him. "No one can't hurt you if you don't let them in."

"No one can love you, either," he said, his voice low in his throat.

"No one would love me anyway."

He turned down the air as she shivered again, looking out the window. "You know, I used to think that, too."

"What's that?"

"That no one could love me." He reached in his pocket and pulled out his wallet, opening it and rubbing a thumb over the photo inside. "Until I met her." It was a small, wrinkled photo of a beautiful Mexican woman. Her bright smile and dark eyes lit up the dull photo. She had one hand wrapped around Logan's neck, their bodies looked as though they had been dancing.

"Who is it?" she asked, trying to look at the photo without him noticing that she cared.

"Her name was Serena."

"Was?"

"Was," he said, not bothering to elaborate.

She nodded. "I'm sorry."

"Me too," he said. "But, my point is that if you open yourself up, sometimes when you least expect it...the right one will come along."

She snorted. "Thanks a lot, *Hallmark.*"

"I'm serious, Fiona. You don't have to keep yourself so shut off and unavailable to the world. The only person you're hurting is yourself."

"I'm not hurting myself. In fact, I'm doing the opposite. Protecting myself is the only thing that matters to me anymore."

"There has to be someone out there you care about."

She swallowed, keeping her eyes straight ahead. "Not anymore."

"But there was once?"

She wasn't sure if it was a question, but she nodded anyway.

"And you got hurt?"

Again, she nodded.

"He was an idiot."

"No," she said softly. "That would be me."

NINE

GIA
SIXTEEN YEARS OLD

The night of her date with Alex came, and Gia was waiting on the front porch for him to arrive. Every noisy truck that came close to her road caused her heart to jump with anticipation, but so far it hadn't been him. Inside the house, Misty was clamoring about, grumbling under her breath about no one caring about her. Rick had left for the afternoon, claiming to be going to watch football, but they all knew that meant he'd be stopping by Richie's bar.

Gia had put a roast in the crockpot, the dishes were done, and the laundry had all been put away. There was quite literally nothing left for Misty to do, but she was adamant about making her daughter feel guilty. Never mind that Gavin and Gunner were both out, and would probably be gone all night, Gia was always the one who was expected to stay home and take care of their mother.

A loud vehicle roared down the road, and she looked up, her eyes locking on his truck as it turned onto her street. He stepped on the gas and then the brakes, squealing his tires in front of her house and rolling down his window. He gave her a dazzling smile, pulling the sunglasses from his face. He didn't mention that he was thirty minutes late, and Gia couldn't bring herself to scold him. Instead, she walked around to the passenger's side and climbed up next to him.

"Hi," she said.

"Hey," he greeted her. "You ready to go?"

She smiled. "Yep."

"I'm glad you decided to come out," he told her as he pulled down her street again.

"Me too," she said, her heart pounding in her chest. She knew this couldn't be reality, too good to be true for her completely ordinary life, and yet she could not stop herself from dreaming of what could be. She couldn't stop imagining the jealous looks she'd get from the girls in school, or the way her mother might be proud of her for finally proving she was worthy of love. She couldn't stop picturing him loving her, running his last name with her first over and over in her head. It was stupid. Completely stupid. But still, she couldn't help it. Alex was the first boy to ever pay attention to her, the first boy to notice her, and she was exhilarated by the confidence his attention was giving her.

When they pulled into Bennie's parking lot just a few minutes later, Alex climbed out of the truck and walked toward the restaurant. Gia climbed out on her side, hurrying to keep up with him. He opened the door, allowing her to walk in first, and she hoped he didn't notice her blush.

He took her hand, pulling her to the corner booth in the

back of the restaurant. A short waitress approached them, smacking her gum loudly. Gia recognized her as Sherry Sias, a girl from Alex's grade. "What can I get ya?" she asked before they could even look at the menu.

"How about an extra order of cheese sticks, Sherry?" Alex asked the waitress, giving her a wink. "With my usual."

She smiled. "You got it, Alex." Gia noticed the way her eyes softened as she stared at him, though they regained their hardness when she stared back at Gia. "What do you want to drink?"

"Oh, just a water is fine," she said softly, looking away.

The girl traipsed off, and Alex's gaze followed her for a moment before looking back at Gia. "You know Sherry?"

She shook her head. "I don't think so."

"She dropped out a few years ago." He held his hands out in front of his belly, pretending to rub a pregnant bump. "Pretty cool in her day, though."

His sentence made Gia feel sick, wondering just how "cool" Sherry had been. She nodded, not sure what to say.

"So," he said, not noticing the tension, "your brothers know you're out with me tonight?"

"No. Why?"

"Just wondering." He smirked. "Gunner isn't my biggest fan."

She grimaced. "Yeah, well, Gunner doesn't control me."

He leaned forward. "Oh yeah? Who does?"

"No one," she said, trying to sound brave. "I do what I want."

He shook his head. "Good. So do I."

"And what is it you want?" she asked, raising an eyebrow, surprised by her own words.

He bit his lip, his eyes dancing between hers. "I'm still trying to work that out."

"Oh?"

"What do you want, Gia?" He touched her hand, running his fingers over hers.

"I don't know if anyone's ever asked me that before."

"Well, I'm asking." He smiled, leaning back.

"I guess I just want to get the hell out of Dale," she said.

"Me too," he admitted.

"Yeah?"

"Yeah. I can't wait to burn some rubber leaving this town and never look back."

It made her sad to think about him leaving, the only person who seemed to care about her. The only friend she had. Besides Gavin. How pathetic was it that her only friend until now was her brother?

"I don't blame you. I'll be right behind you as soon as I can."

He nodded as Sherry appeared with a pepperoni pizza and two orders of cheese sticks. Gia looked at the food, her mouth watering. It was more food than she'd seen in a long time. Even when Rick was working, money was tight, and they were always limited to one helping of whatever food Gia could manage to throw together.

"Dig in," he told her, rubbing his hands together. She picked up a slice, putting it into her mouth cautiously. It was scalding hot, but she couldn't bring herself to care. She was starving, her belly grumbling as the hot food began to fill it. He smiled. "You were hungry, huh?"

She shrugged, still chewing. "I just really love Bennie's."

She'd eaten there only once in her life, but he didn't have to know that.

"Me too," he admitted. "I'll have to remember that for our next date."

Next date. Her insides warmed from more than the pizza at his words, and just like that...she didn't feel so alone.

LATER, *after they'd left Bennie's, Alex surprised her by driving out of town. She rode in silence, wondering where on earth he might be taking her. She hadn't told Misty when she'd be back, but she knew the longer she was gone, the worse her punishment would be. Then again, maybe he was worth it all.*

He pulled up in front of a house she didn't recognize. It was two stories, with tall columns and navy blue shutters. There were people all around, loud music playing. "What is this?" she asked as he opened his door. "I thought we were going to Isaac's?"

"He cancelled, but hey, a party is a party, baby," he said simply. "It's Friday night, and you were planning to be here, right? Daniel's party. I'm sure you were invited."

"Oh, right, yeah, of course."

He held out his hand, lacing his fingers through hers and leading her up the walk. The front door opened and a guy Gia didn't recognize stood in front of them. He held his hand out, giving Alex a quick handshake. "What's up, bro?"

Alex pulled him in, bumping shoulders. "Not much, my man. This is Gia." He gestured toward her. "Gia, this is Daniel."

She smiled. "Hey."

"Come on in, beer's in the back. Aaron's in charge of party favors," he said, touching his nose with a smirk. "Hard liquor's in the den. What's your poison?" he asked Gia.

"Oh, I'm okay, thanks," she said, waving him off.

"Oh, come on," Alex said, leaning into her. "Just one drink? For me?"

She felt her face warming. "Oh, okay, sure."

"Atta girl," he said dotingly. "A beer, then? I'll get it for ya."

She smiled. "Thanks."

He hurried away from her, leaving her standing alone with Daniel. "So, do you go to school in Dale?"

He shook his head. "Not anymore. I graduated a few years ago."

"Oh, wow. Is this your house? It's really nice."

"Yeah," he said. "My parents moved to our winter house in Florida last year. I pretty much have the place all to myself."

She nodded, feeling completely out of place. How in the world was she supposed to relate to anyone whose parents had a "winter house"?

"So, you and Alex, huh? How long's that been going on?"

She crossed her arms, tucking her chin into her chest. "Oh, I don't know if it's...going on. We're just...I mean...I don't know what we are."

"Yeah, I get it. Alex likes to get around," he said with a laugh. "You okay with that?"

She felt her stomach tighten, but before she could answer, Alex was back. He handed her a red cup and took a drink of his own. "What are we talking about, guys?"

"I was just telling Gia I'm glad she could come," Daniel said, turning to look over his shoulder and then disappearing to chase after someone else without a goodbye.

"For what it's worth," Alex told her, "I'm glad you could come, too."

She nodded, taking a sip of her beer. It was disgusting, but she tried to keep her face calm. "Thanks."

"No problem," he said, putting an arm around her shoulder and leading her past the crowd of people. He pushed open a white door and led her into a dark room.

"What are we doing?" she asked nervously.

"Don't worry, I'm just coming in here to chill out for a sec." He flipped on the light, obviously familiar with the room, and walked to the bed. He patted the black and blue plaid comforter, wiggling a finger at her. "Come here." She did as she was told, taking a big gulp of her beer. "Woah, slow down there," he told her, placing his hand over hers on the cup and moving it away from her mouth. "There's plenty of night left."

She swallowed, feeling embarrassed. "I just really love beer."

He laughed softly, taking the cup from her hand and setting it on the nightstand beside them along with his. He turned back to her and her heart sped up, her eyes widening as he put his hand on her cheek, leaning in. She closed her eyes, letting his lips touch hers. She took a deep breath through her nose, breathing in his scent and trying not to panic.

Her first kiss was coming from Alex Donovan. The *Alex Donovan. She put a hand up onto his shoulder, her body shaking with nerves as he leaned in further, his tongue brushing over hers. He began to lie down, easing her down with him. She went, only half aware of what was happening.*

He rolled over, his torso covering hers, one hand cradling her scalp as he stared down at her. He smiled, his lips headed for hers again. Her heart was pounding so fast she was sure it was going to give out. He slid his tongue in her mouth again, this time with more force. His hand left her scalp, moving to her beltline as his fingers crept under her shirt.

She pulled back. "Wait," she said, trying to move her lips from his.

He stared at her. "What's wrong?"

"I...can we just slow down a bit? Please?"

"I thought you wanted to be with me?" he asked, trying to kiss her again.

She pulled back, sitting up so that he was forced off of her. "I do. I just...I really like you, Alex. I do. I just don't want to...do this just yet."

"What are you talking about?"

"Sex," she said, looking down. "I mean, I'm flattered and all, I just...if we could just slow down some." She frowned. "I'm sorry. Is that okay?"

He shook his head. "I can't believe this. You knew what you were signing up for when you agreed to go out with me. Don't even pretend like you didn't. What—did you think I was honestly just going out with you because I thought it'd be fun? You knew this was part of the deal."

"Deal?" she asked, feeling like she'd been slapped. "What deal?"

"I'm Alex Donovan," he said, touching his chest. "The girls I date either put out or get out. Now, come on, Gia, we can have a lot of fun together." He reached for her face again, but she stood up.

"I don't want to do this. I'm sorry. I'd like to go home." And then she added, "Please."

He shook his head, rubbing his jaw and taking a drink of the beer on the nightstand. "My god, what the hell was I thinking with you? Do you even realize who I am? Everyone wants to fuck me. I can walk out of this room right now and have ten girls all lined up and ready for me. Is that what you want? Do you want me to be with someone else tonight?"

She bit her lip. "No, of course not. I just—"

"Just what, Gia? Are you putting out or not? I paid for your food. I took care of you tonight. You owe me this."

She felt cool tears in her eyes, staring at his anger-filled expression. Did she owe him something? He had bought her dinner, after all, and she did know about his reputation when she'd agreed to the date. She'd been stupid to believe he genuinely wanted to date her. She was just another notch on his bedpost. Another conquest. "I'm sorry," she said, wiping a tear from her eye. "Can you please just take me home?"

"Fuck you," he said firmly. "Find your own way home."

"Alex, please," she begged as he stood up and headed for the door. "I don't have a way. We're thirty minutes from Dale." She grabbed hold of his arm.

"You know what you have to do if you want a ride." He stared at her, his brow raised. "Are you up for it, or not?"

She stifled a sob. "I...I can't."

"Then find your own way home. I'm not wasting any more of my time with you." With that, he was out the door and she was left alone, cool tears cascading down her cheeks.

ON MONDAY, *Gia walked into the school to find a note taped to her locker. She unfolded it carefully, staring at the big block letters:* ***WHORE.***

She closed it back, looking around the busy hall. Who could've done this? Who would've had such a horrible thing to say about her? Just then, Rachel Renee and Debi Schmieks walked past, their laughter loud. They stopped a few feet from her and turned around.

Rachel smirked at Gia. "I'm sorry to hear what happened, Gia."

"What?"

"You know." She covered her mouth. "With the..." She made a motion as if she were throwing up. "Alex told everyone. It must've been so embarrassing."

"What are you talking about?"

Debi let out a loud laugh. "Wow, you really did have too much to drink, huh? He told us you gagged on him." She laughed again. "It's okay, Alex is pretty huge. We know from experience. You'll get better."

"If anyone ever lets you try again," Rachel cackled. With that, the girls burst into laughter, covering their mouths and hurrying down the hall.

Gia couldn't believe it. She tossed the note into a nearby trash can and fled to the bathroom. Before she could enter, she saw Alex with a group of his friends. She wanted to go up to him, accuse him of lying, let everyone know how big of a fraud he really was, but she couldn't. He caught her eye over the crowd of people, his expression arrogant. She knew it would be no use to fight him. No use to argue or to tell her version of the events.

Alex Donovan was a god among men, and she was merely

something to be walked on. Someone who might get a bit of sunshine from him as he walked by. Someone who should consider herself lucky he even knew her name. Someone who would be considered lucky for having a chance to be with him. Even if it was for a night. Even if it never even happened.

She shoved open the bathroom door, hurrying past a group of girls staring at themselves in the mirror. She pushed open a stall, locking it behind her just in time for the tears to start falling and her stomach to begin emptying itself. This time, she really was getting sick over Alex Donovan. Just not in the way he'd chosen to take credit for.

TEN

FIONA

Fiona drove down the interstate, the headlights lonely on the empty road. Beside her, Logan sat staring out the window, seemingly lost in his own thoughts. He'd been quiet since they'd stopped for lunch. It had been his suggestion. She was used to going without such frivolous things as meals, but he refused.

Whatever, she thought. If he wanted to spend his money on her, whatever money he had, she wouldn't stop him. After all, she was giving him a ride. It wasn't a warm ride and the company wasn't pleasant, but it was better than walking wherever he was headed. At least she wasn't a serial...no, she couldn't think that anymore. She was a killer, after all. But she wasn't planning to kill him. That's what mattered, right?

He readjusted in his seat, leaning his head back against the headrest. "What's wrong?" he asked her, and she realized she'd been staring at him. She looked back out the windshield, thankful the interstate was so quiet.

"Nothing."

Logan frowned. "So, you never told me where you were headed."

"That's because I don't know."

"You don't have family you want to visit for Thanksgiving?"

She frowned. "What does that have to do with anything?"

"What?"

"Thanksgiving," she said.

He pointed at a billboard up ahead that advertised a Thanksgiving special. "You do realize next month is Thanksgiving, right?"

She frowned. "Oh. No, I hadn't thought about it."

"Hadn't thought about it? Are you not a big fan of Thanksgiving?"

She looked down, feeling uncomfortable. She didn't need Logan's pity. Not about her past, not about her life now. She didn't want to tell him that she'd never celebrated Thanksgiving aside from the dinners they'd have in her classrooms. She didn't want to tell him that one time she had asked her mother why they didn't celebrate Thanksgiving like the rest of her classmates, and Misty had replied that they had nothing to be thankful for. So, instead, she shook her head. "Nope, not a huge fan."

He shook his head. "That's just because you've never celebrated it the right way."

"What's the right way?"

He shrugged. "With my cooking."

"You cook?"

He nodded. "My mother was a chef. She taught me everything she knew."

"Was?" she asked, noticing the sadness in his voice.

"She passed away a few years ago. Alzheimer's."

"I'm sorry," she said. And she was. She found herself feeling sorry for Logan, though she rarely felt sorry for anyone.

"It's okay," he told her.

"Were you two close?"

He nodded. "We lost touch as I got older, but at one point, yes. She was one of my best friends."

Fiona couldn't relate, but she did know what it was like to lose a best friend. After all, Holly had been the only friend she'd ever really known. When they'd been paired up for a class project, Fiona had been furious. How on earth was she supposed to work with one of the richest, most popular kids in her class? How could they possibly find anything in common? But, they had. Holly had been one of the most down-to-earth girls she'd ever met. Over time, she'd grown to consider her a friend. Her only friend. Then came Fletcher. From the moment Fletcher laid eyes on Holly, Fiona knew it was over. Holly would choose Fletcher over her, and why shouldn't she? Fletcher was certainly more fun. He knew how to interact with people. He wasn't awkward. He was allowed to be outside the house much more than she was. It just made sense. But still, Fiona had begged him not to date Holly. He could date any girl he'd wanted, and yet Holly was *the* girl he'd wanted. And once they'd begun dating, Fiona was forgotten about. Slowly, Holly stopped spending any time with her. When she was around, Fletcher was too. It just wasn't the same. And eventually Fiona conceded.

Stepping back from the friendship entirely. So, yes, though she couldn't relate to losing, or caring about losing, a mother, she certainly knew the sting of a lost friendship.

"What about you?" he asked, interrupting her thoughts. "You and your parents? Were you close?"

She laughed, a snort ripping from her throat. "No."

"No, you weren't close?"

"No," she said again. "We weren't...we weren't close."

"I'm sorry to hear that."

"Don't be," she said. "It doesn't bother me."

"Of course it does," he said.

She lowered her brow. "You don't know anything about me."

"No, but I know human nature. It's normal to crave closeness with our parents. Studies show kids who have normal relationships with their parental figures are more likely to feel confident in their relationships with others. Plus, they're more likely to be able to hold a steady job and contribute to society. So much of who you become goes back to who you are raised by. It's the whole nature versus nurture thing—"

"What the hell are you talking about?" she asked, turning to look at him in the dark car. "How do you know all of that?"

He looked away, getting quiet. "Sorry. It just...it all interests me."

Fiona looked back to the road. "You're so weird." He laughed. "What's funny?"

"Nothing," he said. "You're right. I am weird. But, I think you're pretty weird too." She frowned. "Are you going to ask why I think you're weird?"

"No. I am weird. Why should I care what you think?"

He pointed out the window. "We should stop here for the night."

"The Four Seasons?"

"Yeah, why? Do you have something against it?"

"Yeah," she said bitterly. "I prefer winter."

He smiled. "I'll turn the thermostat down."

"Seriously, it's way too expensive. What the hell do you do for a living?"

"I thought you didn't want to know anything about each other."

"No, I don't want you to know anything about me. And I don't want you to think we're friends and you should just start spilling your guts to me. But I do want to know how you've got so much money."

"Are you worried I'm a criminal?"

She smiled. "I'd be more worried if you weren't."

"Well, I guess you should worry, then. I'm not a criminal."

"But you are on the run from something?"

He shook his head as she turned onto the exit he'd directed her toward. "You get one question. For now. Do you want to know how I got my money or if I'm on the run?"

"I want to know both."

"You have to choose," he said, a challenging look on his face.

"Fine. I want to know if you're on the run."

"You already know the answer to that," he said.

"You are."

"Mhm," he said with a quick nod. "Just like you."

"Why?"

"That's two questions."

"It's one and a half." She turned onto the next street, headed for the hotel. The city's downtown was busy and she tightened her grip on the wheel as she switched lanes, prepared to turn at the next light.

"Fine. I'll give you half an answer then. I'm on the run because of my job."

"What...are you like a spy?"

He shook his head, his mop of hair bouncing. "No."

"What then?"

"That's officially the end of our questions for the time being," he said as she turned at the light and pulled into the hotel's lot. "Let the valet park us."

"No way," she said. "I park myself."

"Fine," he said, not arguing. "Park then and let's get out. I'm starving."

For such a skinny man, he ate more than Fiona had thought possible. Then again, she was so unused to any sort of eating schedule, maybe he was eating the normal amount. She parked the car in the far lot and stepped out, walking to the trunk to grab her bag. Logan pulled his own from the trunk and turned to walk inside.

"I'm just getting us one room," he said over his shoulder.

"What? Why?"

"Why not?" he asked, walking through the doors as the bellhops greeted them. "You'll just end up in my room anyway."

ELEVEN

FIONA

Fiona walked into the hotel room, a room the size of a large, two bedroom apartment by her standards. "Woah," she said, her breath taken away as she stared around the room. It was gorgeous with tall, sculpted ceilings and beautiful artwork. She could never have dreamed of staying in a place like this. Hell, she could have never dreamed of *peeing* in a place like this.

She set her bag down on the end of the bed, walking to the window and staring out at the city skyline. "This is..."

"Beautiful," he finished her thought, walking too close behind her. She spun around, moving so she was no longer in between him and the window. "I always loved coming here."

"You've been here before?" she asked.

"I used to travel a lot. For work."

"Right...back when you were a...partner at a law firm?" she guessed.

"Nope." He shook his head, placing a hand on the glass. "Good try." She stood, watching him look out over the city. "It seems like another life now," he said, barely more than a whisper.

"Do you miss it?" she asked.

"Every day," he said, a sad smile on his face as he turned to stare at her. "What about you? Do you miss your old life?"

"No," she said firmly. "I'm glad it's over."

"That bad, huh?"

She looked down. "I'm not good at...this."

"What's this?"

"Talking to...well, anyone really. Talking about how I feel. *Knowing* how I feel, for that matter. I'm just, I'm not good."

"You don't have to be, Fiona," he told her, moving a finger to lift up her chin so their eyes met. She pulled away, taking a step back, but didn't avert her gaze. "We can figure this out together. You don't have to be good at it. I'm definitely not going to be good at it. But, I can listen if you want to talk. I can hold you if you need to cry. I'm—"

"I don't," she interrupted him. "I don't cry."

"Everyone cries," he said. "There's no shame in—"

"I don't. I can't."

"What do you mean?"

She shook her head, her eyes wide. "There's something wrong with me."

"Someone really hurt you." He let out a sigh through his nose, his lips pressed together.

"No," she said. "Everyone really hurt me."

TWELVE

GIA

TEN YEARS OLD

It was summer. Gia ran through her grandparents' lake house at top speed. "Gavin, give it back!" she screamed, trying desperately to pull the journal from her brother's hand.

He let out a laugh. "Why? You don't want me to find out who you have a crush on?" He opened the purple diary, beginning to read aloud. "Dear Diary, today in class—"

"Now, that's about enough," their grandmother's sharp voice rang through the room. She walked toward them quickly. "What is going on?"

"He took my journal, Grandma," she tattled. "Make him give it back."

"Gavin," their grandmother held out her hand, "give the journal back to your sister."

He scoffed. "Why can't she just learn to take a joke?" he

asked, tossing the journal back to her so it thudded against her chest.

"It's not funny," she spat, holding the book carefully. "Leave my stuff alone."

"Whatever," Gavin said, turning to walk from the room.

Her grandmother looked down at her. "You know he's just doing it to get a rise from you, sweetheart."

"He thinks he's funny."

"You guys have got to get along. One day, you'll be all each other has."

"No way, as soon as I'm eighteen, I'm running away and never looking back."

"You say that now," she said with a kind smile, moving to sit down on the couch and patting the seat next to her. "But, one day, when I'm gone—"

"You won't ever be gone, Grandma."

"Someday I will," she said, "and so will Grandpa and your parents, and you guys will have to look out for each other."

"The boys hate me," she said. "They just pick on me."

"That's because they're your brothers. It's what they do best. But, it doesn't mean they hate you. In fact, it means the opposite. Your brothers love you so much, Gia," she said, rubbing the girl's cheek. "You just watch...if anyone ever tries to hurt you...those boys will be the first in line to protect you. They'll take care of you. Just like you'll take care of them."

She stuck out her tongue, pretending to be disgusted, when in reality the idea of someone, anyone, *protecting her sounded quite nice.*

"Well, I still want to get away when I'm old enough," she said finally. "So, I won't be around to take care of them."

"You should. You should get far away from here, Gia. Explore. Live. Go to the corners of the world and meet new people and eat new foods and learn new things. That's what life's all about, my sweet. I hope that's exactly what you do. But, that doesn't mean you have to lose touch with your brothers."

"I won't ever get to explore the world. Not like that."

"Why do you say that?"

"It's too expensive. We'll never have that kind of money," she said. Even at ten years old, Gia had a vast understanding of money, or rather, a lack thereof. Misty had made sure of that.

Her grandmother pulled her into a hug, kissing her forehead. "I don't want you to worry about that. You'll be just fine."

"No, I won't. Gunner says we'll all end up just like Mom and Dad. Stuck in Dale forever."

"Gia," she said, pulling her granddaughter's face into her hands. "I'm going to tell you something I don't want you to repeat to your brothers, okay?"

"Okay. What is it?"

"Your grandfather and I, we've got money set aside for you. For after we're gone. We want to make sure you're taken care of and that you can get out, if that's what you want."

"Really?" she asked, her eyes widening at the possibility.

"Yes, really. It's all set up in your name already. We've willed everything to you."

"Just me?"

She tapped her nose. "Just you. Now, don't go getting any crazy ideas. I fully expect that you'll take that money and use it to help your brothers as well, but I promised my mother that I would pass our money along to my first born daughter."

"Mom?"

"Yes," she said, "but after she married your father, your grandfather and I rewrote our will. We set up a trust in your name after you were born. It was important to my mother that our family's money stay with the women. It's the way it's always been. And it's how I'll expect you to do, too. When the time comes. That doesn't mean you can't help out your brothers, because like I said, you should, but it does mean that you're who I'm trusting with our money. Money that I have worked hard for, and my mother and her mother before that. Our family legacy will be in your hands someday, my sweet Gia, and the world will be at your fingertips."

"Is it a lot of money?" she asked, her face growing warm.

Her grandmother chuckled. "It's enough, but you have to promise me you won't let that go to your head. There's nothing more satisfying than a hard day's work, Gia. That's something your mother never learned. I pray every day you don't follow in her footsteps. If you choose to join the company someday, you'll not only double or even triple the money we've put back for you, but you'll take pride knowing you contributed. You did something with your life. There's nothing, no amount of money or fame, that could ever surpass that."

"Does Momma know?" she asked. "That you wrote her out of the will, I mean."

"Yes," she said, her lips tight. "Yes, she does. And, I'm sure you know she isn't happy about it. When the time comes, when we pass away, she will try to fight with all she has to get the money, but our lawyer has assured us she has no claim to

it. We've written out iron-proof clauses that make it so you'll never have to worry about anything happening to your money."

She nodded. "It feels weird. Taking your money. Calling it mine."

"Well, it won't be until we die. And you'll have to be eighteen. But, then it will belong to you. I want you to feel free to do what you want with your life, without being burdened or brought down by your mother's choices."

"Is that why she hates me?" she asked, feeling the words catch in her throat.

"Hates you?" her grandmother asked in horror. "Oh, sweetheart, she doesn't hate you." She pulled her into another hug, stroking her hair. "I know your mother can be a little cold and your father is...well—" She stopped, biting her lip. "The point is, she doesn't hate you. She just...she's lost right now, Gia. She's not the woman we raised anymore. Most days, I don't know who she is. But, she loves you. She loves all three of you so much." She kissed her head. "And so do I."

Gia hugged her back. "I love you too, Grandma."

"Ewww, love fest in here," Gavin called, cackling as he walked back through the room, covering his eyes.

"Shut up, Gavin," she yelled.

"You shut up, Gia," he said, sticking his tongue out.

"Both of you shut up," their grandfather said, walking into the room with a can of whipped cream. "Or you aren't getting ice cream." He winked at them, turning back to walk into the kitchen. Gia jumped off the couch, feeling a little bit lighter. Some of the weight she'd been doomed to carry had lifted. At least for the moment.

THIRTEEN

FIONA

Fiona flipped through the channels mindlessly, searching for a show she might recognize. Most of it was foreign to her, though she had been allowed to watch TV during the time she was in the clinic. None of it stuck out to her anyway, with the way her mind was always wandering.

She thought back to her doctor, to Neville, the last man she'd been alone with like she was alone with Logan. But, it had been different with Neville. Neville wanted things from her. Neville wanted to be with her. What was it that Logan wanted? She didn't quite know.

So far, he'd been extremely generous, offering much more than he asked for in return, but she'd never be so naïve to think that would last long. She knew the time would come when he'd expect reimbursement for his kindness. What would he want that she could possibly have to give? Besides the obvious. And she couldn't do that. Not with Logan. Not in exchange for what he'd given her. She'd sworn to herself she wouldn't sleep with men to get ahead anymore. It was killing her. The men she'd been with, the things she'd been through, all for a meal to get through the week or a bit of gas to get an exit further, they haunted her just as much as her mother's harsh hands and sharp tongue.

No. When the time came, she would have to turn her back on him. If she made it that long, anyway.

The door swung open, and her thoughts were interrupted. Logan stood in front of her, and she gasped. He was wearing a black suit and tie, his messy hair had been tamed, and he held a white, floor-length bag over his arm.

"Logan? What are you—"

"I guessed at your size," he told her, laying the bag on the bed. "Now hurry up, we're running late."

"Late for what?" she asked, staring at the bag.

"Thanksgiving," he told her, a wide grin on his face.

"What are you talking about? Thanksgiving isn't for another month."

"I know. But we may not be together then."

"Why wouldn't we?"

"Just go with me on this, okay?"

"Why should I?" she challenged.

"Because I can guarantee you this will be the best Thanksgiving you've ever had."

"I've already told you I hate Thanksgiving. I've never had a good one."

"Well, it shouldn't be hard then, should it?" He gestured toward the bag. "Go on. Get dressed."

"I'm not hungry."

"We both know that's not true."

"Well, even if it's not, I'm not dressing up. I hate dresses."

"Come on," he said. "For me? Please? Just one night. One dress. All the food you can eat."

She sighed. "Why do I have to dress up? Can't we just eat in our room?"

"Because it's important to me."

"Why should I care what's important to you? I'm not doing you any favors."

"I didn't say it was *for* me. I said it's important to me. It's for you."

She cocked her head to the side. "You've lost your mind."

He nodded. "Yeah, I'm pretty sure I have. But, maybe it's worth it."

"I'm gonna need more words than that."

"Can you just...can you just please get dressed? I'll explain all of it at dinner." He paused, staring at her with his dreamy, pleading eyes. "Please?"

She sighed, grabbing the bag. "Fine," she said, storming to the bathroom. "But only because I'm starving."

A FEW MINUTES LATER, Fiona had pulled the blue dress on, surprised by how well it fit her. Sure, it was a bit loose, but all in all, he hadn't done bad. She stepped into the black heels he'd given her and placed a clip in her hair. It wasn't great. In fact, she still looked pretty homeless, but it was the best she'd felt in years. She'd always hated dresses, that much was true, but standing there now, in front of the mirror, she couldn't bring herself to hate this dress. It was too beautiful. The man had taste, she had to give him that.

She opened the bathroom door, walking out into the room with her head down, trying not to trip. She hadn't walked in heels in well over ten years.

Logan stood from the bed, a whistle escaping his lips. "You look amazing," he said, staring at her in awe.

"Thank you," she said with a smile. "Now, let's go."

He nodded, walking past her quickly to open the door. He held it open for her, his eyes still locked with hers, though she pulled her gaze away quickly. "Thank you."

They walked to the elevator in silence. Once they'd stepped in, he pressed the button for the lobby, and she sighed. "So, are you going to tell me where you're taking me? I feel like we're going to be overdressed." She was worried he'd be taking her to a restaurant filled with rich and snobby people. A place where people like Logan might fit in, but she would not. They'd see through the expensive dress right away, see her for the impostor that she was. She could never fit in with Logan's crowd. Her throat was dry just thinking of it.

"Oh, I've got someplace special in mind."

As the elevator doors opened, Logan held out his arm for her, waiting until she begrudgingly wrapped hers through it. "I don't know if I like special, Logan."

"Maybe you just haven't experienced my kind of special."

She smiled, feeling warmth flood her cheeks. "Who says I want to?"

"You're here, aren't you?" he asked, stopping in front of a heavy double door. He grabbed hold of the golden handle, pulling it open and causing her to gasp. The dark ballroom was lit by blue-colored lights. Large, sweeping curtains, chandeliers, and candles filled the room, making it dream-like. He stepped in, watching her expression. Though she wanted so badly to keep her usual hard expression, she couldn't hold back the wonder that filled her eyes.

"What is this place? This is what you've been working on all day?" she asked, staring at the ornate ceiling in awe. She glanced down, meeting his eyes. The floor was completely empty except for a single table, set with a white fabric table-cloth, two chairs, and a single lily in a vase.

He dropped his arm, pulling out a chair and letting her sit down. She reached up, touching the flower with an outstretched finger. "You didn't seem like a rose kind of girl," he said, taking a seat across from her.

"No one's ever gotten me flowers before," she whispered, her voice feeling shaky. How was it possible the effect he had on her? She hadn't consciously allowed him to get any closer to her than anyone else, so how was it possible that he had? That he could make her feel this way. That he could make her feel at all.

Staring at him, in the dimly lit room, it was as if she were a teenager again, giddy over a boy who would destroy her. He must've noticed the way her eyes went dark, because he frowned, reaching across the table and touching her hand. To both of their surprises, she didn't pull away. "Don't go there," he said softly.

"Where?" she asked, lowering her brow.

"Wherever you go when you start to shut me out. That place in your head that makes you think you can't trust me. Just...just don't go there tonight. Stay with me. Let me in."

She shook her head. "I can't, Logan...I just—"

"Don't think about it. Just be here with me tonight."

"It's not that simple."

"So, we make it that simple. For tonight. We'll take it one day at a time."

"I don't know how to do that," she said, looking away.

He touched her hand again. "I'll help you." She looked back at him, feeling so vulnerable and yet so safe all at once. "I'll help you, Fiona. If you let me."

She nodded, though she couldn't speak. Just then, music began playing overhead, and the doors at the far end of the room opened. A man in a chef's hat entered the room, pushing a cart loaded with food. He approached them, a smile on his face, and stopped in front of their table. "Dinner is served," he said, setting two plates in front of each of them. Fiona looked down, the plates loaded up with traditional Thanksgiving food. He pulled out two more plates, pies and brownies on them, and set them in the middle of the table. It was more food than Fiona had ever seen, more food than she could even dream about eating. "Enjoy." With that, the man walked away.

Fiona picked up the fork in front of her, taking a bite of the stuffing.

"Mhmm," she groaned. "Oh my god, this is delicious."

Logan picked up his own fork, taking a bite as well. "I told you I would have you liking Thanksgiving."

"But it's not Thanksgiving. Technically, you have me liking October twenty-third."

"Just admit it, I've given you a reason to like Thanksgiving."

She took another bite. "You are just determined to prove me wrong."

"I like to be right," he said plainly.

"Well, I dislike the experiences of Thanksgiving, or rather, the fact that I have no experience with Thanksgiving, not the food."

"Well, this Thanksgiving is going to change all of that," he said, locking eyes with her. "I'm going to change all of that."

"Why?" she asked, rubbing her fork over the potatoes.

"Why?"

"Yes, why? Why do you care so much? About trying to...to fix me. Or make me better. Happier. Whatever."

"I'm not trying to make you *better,* Fiona. Or to fix you. I do want you to be happier, because that's what you hope for the people you care about."

"Why do you care about me?"

"Because someone needs to." His words shocked her, his gaze never faltering as he continued to stare at her. He took another bite, chewing slowly. "And because you need to know that you're worth caring about."

She closed her eyes, pushing back away from the table and standing up. Her head was pounding, her heart thudding loudly in her chest. It was as if she couldn't catch her breath. She hurried away from him, cool tears forming in her eyes. Why on earth was she crying? She hadn't lied when she said she didn't cry. The feeling was so unfamiliar it was as if it were a new sensation totally. She wiped her eyes, feeling his warm hands on her shoulders. "Fiona?"

She refused to look his way, angry at her own tears. She had built the wall around herself for a reason, and this was it. She hated feeling this way, open and exposed. It was unnatural to her. He spun her around slowly. "Fiona," he whispered, pulling her into his arms, "what's wrong?"

She shook her head, going stiff as he wrapped his arms around her, her face finding a bit of comfort in his chest. He slid his arm down hers, pulling her clenched hand away from her chest and holding it gently. He put one hand on her waist, beginning to sway to the music, his breath in her ear. "Shhh," he whispered, comforting her. "It's okay. It's all going to be okay."

She was silent, focusing on her breathing, her own warm breath bouncing off his chest and back to her face. There were small tears on his jacket, and she worried she'd ruined it. Like she ruined everything else. He laid his cheek on hers, his thumb stroking her knuckles. "One step at a time," he whispered. "You don't have to do anything or feel anything you aren't ready for."

But, what choice did she have when her heart wasn't listening? When her head was being overpowered by the terrifying feeling of love in her chest? She was helpless to stop it. Hopeless. She couldn't control her feelings anymore, and that wasn't okay with her. Nothing about this was okay.

"Logan, I...I—"

"You what, Fiona? Talk to me."

"I'm scared," she said, relief washing over her as more tears poured out.

He pulled back, staring into her eyes. "What are you scared of?"

"Nothing. Everything. I don't know."

"Name one thing. One thing you're scared of. We'll work through it."

"I'm terrified of caring about you."

"Do you?" he asked.

She shook her head. "I don't want to."

"That's not what I asked."

"But it's the answer I can give."

"You deserve happiness, Fiona. You know that, right?"

"No," she said simply. "I don't."

"What makes you say that?"

"I know who I am, Logan. I know what I've done, and I make no apologies for it. But, I don't deserve happiness. I don't deserve anything anymore."

"What have you done that's so terrible?" He brushed a piece of hair from her eyes.

"I can't tell you that."

"Because you don't trust me?"

"No," she said. "I don't trust you, but that's not the reason."

"What is the reason?"

She looked down, then back up slowly. "Because I don't ever want you to stop looking at me like that."

He lowered his brow, his lips parting. "I don't know if that's possible." He leaned in carefully, his eyes on hers as their mouths drew closer together. The tension around them grew, and she pulled away before his skin touched hers.

He pulled back. If he was embarrassed, he didn't let it show. "Fiona, I'm not perfect. I've made mistakes. I've done horrible things. I don't want you to be perfect...I just want you to be you."

"You don't know what you're asking. The *me* who I've become is a monster."

"I know you believe that. I can see how deeply you do, but I just can't see how it can be true. When I look into your eyes, I see goodness. I see someone who's scared. Someone who's been told she's not good enough for so long she's started to believe it herself."

"I'm not—"

"You are," he said firmly. "You are good. You are worthy, Fiona. You don't have to do anything special in this life in order to be worthy of love. You *are* just by existing. That's all you have to do." He smiled. "And look how good at existing you are."

She put her head on his chest. "How are you so good with me?"

He kissed the top of her head, her skin burning at his touch. "Because underneath it all, we're not that different. I'm just as scared and broken as you are. I'm just a little better at hiding it."

"You don't seem broken."

He nodded. "I'm an expert at not seeming broken."

"What happened?" she asked.

"I lost someone very special to me. More than one someone, actually. And...in doing so, I just about lost myself."

"Selena?" she asked, recalling the name of the woman in the photograph.

"Yes," he said, "Selena."

"How did she die?"

He shook his head. "I don't mind telling you. But, for tonight, I'd rather just enjoy our time together. One night of happiness. All the darkness will be here tomorrow."

"It never leaves."

"I can fix that," he whispered, leaning in again, this time quicker so that their lips met before she could comprehend it. The air around them froze, the room seeming to fall silent, though she knew the music was still playing. Her heart pounded, adrenaline coursing through her so her whole body was on edge. She wanted so badly to resist, wanted to pull away, to tell him no, but she couldn't. Deep down, below the fear, was an insurmountable feeling of pure joy. So sweet and warm that it filled her belly instantly, making her crave more.

He placed a hand over her cheek, cupping her face. His kiss was soft and comforting, their lips fitting together perfectly. And just like that, as quickly as it started, it was over. Logan pulled back, tucking a piece of hair behind her ears. He offered her a small smile.

She took a deep breath, pressing her lips together, wanting desperately to touch his lips again. "Did you really rent this whole ballroom for us?" She looked around the room, trying to fill the silence.

"I did."

"That must've been expensive," she said.

"It was." He nodded, then grinned. "It was worth it."

"But how? You didn't spend all your money?"

"No," he whispered. "Not all of it." He looked down. "I don't want you to worry about it, Fiona. I told you, I'll take care of you." He moved his arm back to her waist, beginning to dance again.

She laid her head against his shoulder, trying to calm her racing heart. "This feels strange."

He laughed. "Well, you certainly know how to deflate a guy's ego."

She squeezed his hand. "Good strange," she admitted. "Just...strange."

"It gets easier," he whispered, kissing her forehead.

She lifted her head to stare at him. "What does?"

"Pretending that everything's okay."

"How long have you been pretending?"

"Since the day Selena died." He sighed. "About three months ago."

She frowned. "Oh."

"How about you? How long has it been for you?"

She felt a small tear fall down her cheek again and brushed it away. "I've been pretending my whole life."

FOURTEEN

GIA
SEVENTEEN YEARS OLD

Gia rushed through the party, a drink in her hand. She'd failed her chemistry test that morning and was wallowing a bit. Not that she'd be in trouble; Misty didn't care and Rick would never remember to ask, but she'd stayed up late the night before to study. She thought she had it down but failed miserably. Gia knew passing her classes was the only way she'd be allowed to get a scholarship and make it out of Dale. And, at this rate, that wasn't going to happen. It wasn't her fault she had so many chores to do before she was ever allowed to study. It wasn't her fault she could hear her parents fighting through her door, making it hard to focus on her studies. It wasn't her fault the boys would leave, making it her responsibility to deal with Misty's rage and their father's drunken mess. It wasn't her fault, and yet it had become her life.

She took another drink, searching for the bathroom. Gia

didn't spend much time at parties, they weren't traditionally her scene. Though Gavin had taken to following Rick's footsteps, drinking and partying every chance he had, Gia wanted to be nothing like either of her parents. She wanted to be better. Still, she was allowed one night to let in the self-pity, right?

She found the bathroom, finally, and rushed inside, flipping on the light. She stared into the mirror as she unbuttoned her pants, at the wild, dark hair and empty brown eyes that always awaited her. She closed her eyes, sitting down and relieving her bladder. When she was finished, she stood up, washing her hands quickly and walking back out of the room without another look at herself.

She ran straight into someone, bounding back and gasping. "Oh, sorry," she said, apologizing before she saw him. Alex stared down at her, a sly smile growing on his face.

"Gia," he said, "hey."

She grimaced, trying to hurry past him, not bothering to respond.

He grabbed hold of her arm. "Wait," he said, letting it go as she spun around to face him. "Don't run off."

"I have nothing to say to you," she said, stepping back from him.

"I know," he said, nodding. "I know I was a jerk."

"That's an understatement."

He smirked. "I know, Gia. I know and I'm sorry. I was an idiot with a wounded ego, and I can't say I'm sorry enough." He moved to touch her hair, and she smacked his hand away. "Look," he said softly, "I know I have no right to ask this...but can we just talk? Please?"

"Why? What could you possibly have to say to me?"

He pointed toward a door at the end of the hall. "Can we go in there?" he asked.

"Yeah, right," she said with a loud laugh. "You must think I'm a moron. I wouldn't be caught dead alone with you ever again."

"I'm not going to hurt you, Gia. I just want to talk."

"So, talk, Alex. I'm not going anywhere with you. I don't trust you. I'm sure you can understand why."

He sighed, rubbing his forehead. "I just...I just wanted you to know how sorry I am. You were a nice girl, and I had no right to treat you the way that I did. I really liked you, and I was hurt when you turned me down." He frowned, lowering his voice. "I'm not really used to being told no."

"Yeah, you made that abundantly clear."

"But it gave me no right to do what I did."

"To do what you did? Do you mean leaving me stranded and alone so that I had to call my brother to come and pick me up from a town away? Or were you talking about the rumors that you started? The fact that I'm now one of Dale's biggest whores and I've barely had my first kiss? Do you know how many notes I've had taped to my locker? The horrible things people whisper about me when I walk past? I'm fine, Alex, trust me, I've dealt with worse. But school was somewhere I could be invisible. Somewhere I could feel safe. You took that from me. You took away the only safe place I had. I will never forgive you for that." She closed her eyes. "So, if you'll excuse me..."

"I'm an idiot," he said, stepping out of her way.

"Agreed." She marched past him.

He followed her. "But I really am sorry, Gia. I'm going to prove that to you."

"Good luck with that." She tossed her drink into a nearby trash can and stormed from the house, no longer wanting anything to do with the party.

THE NEXT DAY AT SCHOOL, *Alex was waiting at her locker. "Hey," he greeted her, handing her a white paper cup.*

"What's this?" she asked, staring at it.

"Coffee," he said simply, taking a drink of his own.

"Where did you get coffee?"

"Teacher's lounge." She stared at him but didn't bother asking how he managed to get anything from the only room in the building where students weren't allowed.

"I don't drink coffee." She reached up, spinning the lock and opening her locker.

"Fine," he said, taking the cup back and tossing it into the trash so that some spilled down the side. He placed one hand in his letterman jacket pocket. "Can I walk you to class?"

"I can't stop you," she said, slamming her locker shut and turning away.

He moved closer, keeping stride with her. "What class do you have next?"

"Health," she told him.

"Finals?"

She nodded.

"Boy, am I not going to miss those," he teased.

"You aren't going to college?"

"Yeah, probably on a football scholarship. Jocks don't need brains, right?"

"You've made it this far without them."

He let out a laugh. "I never noticed that attitude before."

"You hadn't pissed me off before," she said firmly.

"Well, lucky for you, I'll be graduating soon and you won't have to deal with me." He was joking, she knew, but she didn't smile. Instead, she rounded the corner toward the hall where her next class was. "So, are you ready to forgive me yet?"

"Yes, you found the magic cure, Alex. I've totally forgotten about everything and am ready to fall madly in love with you," she said, her tone monotonous.

"I know you're joking," he said, stopping in front of her classroom and locking eyes with her, "but I'm not."

"I told you I'm not going to forgive you, and I meant it. So, just please leave me alone." With that, she disappeared into her classroom without looking back.

IN MAY, *Gia accompanied Gavin and Holly to her older sister's graduation. Partly because she was looking forward to spending time with Holly again, even if she was playing third-wheel, but partly because she just wanted to get out of the house. Misty had been particularly moody since Rick had lost his job. Again.*

After graduation, Holly invited her to join them at a party on the outskirts of town. Gia didn't particularly like the idea of going to any parties, seeing as how they'd been less than fond memories for her, but she was enjoying seeing Holly and she hated to let the girl she considered to be her only friend down. So, begrudgingly, she agreed.

When they arrived at the party, Gia immediately saw Alex and groaned. Holly wrapped an arm through hers, pulling her through the doorway and past him before he could say a word. Holly had no idea what had gone down between them, but Gia was sure she'd heard the rumors just like everyone. She was intensely grateful for her friend's protective and fearless nature in that moment. Alex hardly glanced at them as they passed.

Gavin was a few steps behind them, high-fiving and chatting with people as they made their way through the room. That was her brother, forever comfortable and able to find friends in any setting. People flocked to Gavin, he made them feel at ease, it was no different with her. He just had that effect. Gia was the opposite. She made people feel the awkwardness around them; she was no good at small talk or making people feel comfortable. It was why she had once gotten along with Holly so well, Holly saw past the awkwardness. It didn't faze her. She was like Gavin in that she could make friends anywhere with anyone.

Gavin located a table with the drinks, bringing them each a cup and taking one for himself. "Next year, this will be us," he said loudly, looking around at all the happy seniors. "Here's to the best year of our lives."

The girls bounced their cups against his, taking drinks and smiling happily. It was impossible to be in a bad mood around Gavin. His positivity was contagious. Holly groaned. "My lame sister has no idea how lucky she is. She just graduated. And I guarantee whatever she's doing right now has nothing to do with packing her bags to get the hell out of this town."

"I have a few guesses about what she's doing," Gavin said with a laugh, wiggling his eyebrows. "I don't see Gunner around here, do you?"

Holly made a disgusted face. "Thanks for that mental image. My point is that she should be preparing to run out of town as fast as her car will carry her. But, no, she's going to stay in Dale. Probably for the rest of her life. Look at all of these people." She took another drink. "If that were me, I'd be long gone."

Gavin pulled her into a kiss. "When that's us, we will be long gone."

Gia looked at them. "You're planning to leave?"

"Yeah," Gavin said, still hugging Holly. "Aren't you?"

"Well, yeah, of course. I just...I didn't think about you leaving together."

"What's wrong?" Gavin asked, studying her expression.

"Nothing," she said, taking a drink quickly. She wasn't going to say what was on her mind...that the idea of losing her brother was enough to make her break down right there. Sure, Gavin drove her nuts, but most days he was the closest thing she had to a friend. As much as she'd always planned to leave, the idea of losing Gavin, of leaving without him, terrified her.

"Oh, hey, I wanna go talk to Jessica for a second," Holly said, pointing to her friend across the room. She kissed Gavin's cheek, waving to Gia rather than inviting her along. "I'll be back."

As she disappeared, Gavin looked to his sister. "You'll be okay, right?" he asked.

"Here?" Sure. Even though you're the reason I'm here.

"No, when I leave." He stared at her then, and she realized he knew her expression all too well.

"I'll be fine, Gav," she said, patting his arm.

"It's still a year away."

"I know that."

"It's not like I'll be abandoning you," he said, his voice soft.

"Gavin, I'm fine. I swear I'm fine." She was lying through her teeth and they both knew it, but he nodded.

"I love you, G-G," he teased, calling her by her childhood nickname.

She rolled her eyes. "Shut up."

He laughed, taking another drink before crushing his cup. "I'm gonna go find Holly, okay?" he said, staring across the room at her. "You'll be okay, yeah?"

She nodded. "Sure. I'm fine."

He nodded. "I'll catch you later."

She turned away from him, looking over her shoulder as he disappeared before she directed her attention back in front of her. She looked around the party, seeing so many familiar faces, and yet no one she felt she could cling to. She shook her head. She had been stupid for coming. Stupid for believing somehow this party would give her a friend again. Of course it wouldn't. She saw Holly across the room, talking happily with her friend, smiling wildly as Gavin approached. It hurt Gia. Of course it did. It was incredibly obvious that she was out of place here.

She closed her eyes, headed for the door. She could find her way home. They were still in Dale, after all. At most it'd be a twenty-minute walk home. She could make it.

She hurried through the crowded room, darting in between people before she finally reached her escape. She swung open the door and stared into a familiar face. "Woah, slow down," Daniel Kindall said, holding out a hand to stop her. "What's the rush?"

She pushed his hand from her shoulder. "Get out of my way."

"Wait, is everything okay?" he asked, lowering his face so he was eye level with her.

She looked down. "I just have somewhere else to be."

He brushed a piece of her hair back from her eyes. "You're Alex's friend, right? The one who came to my party before?"

She bit her lip, not wanting to claim Alex as anything, certainly not a friend. "I was at your party for a bit, yeah."

"I thought you looked familiar," he said, smirking. "You sure you're all right?"

"Yeah, I just need to get home," she said, trying to move past him.

He stepped in front of her again. "Where's your car?"

"I don't live far from here."

"Wait, so you're walking?"

"Yeah," she said simply. "I'm walking."

"Do you want a ride?"

"No. I'm fine." She frowned. "Thanks though."

"Yeah, of course," he said. "Are you sure? I don't mind. It's late. You probably shouldn't be walking alone."

"I can take care of myself."

He chuckled, finally stepping back from her. "I'm sure you can. I just wanted to make sure you were safe."

She took a step past him without another word, walking down the long, paved walkway, and headed for the street. She clenched her fists to her sides, walking past a car with steamed up windows and another with two guys from her class smoking pot. They didn't notice her. No one did. It was just a fact.

Most days, Gia could move in and out of her day completely invisible. That was, until Alex started the rumors. The lies. The rumors that had suddenly put her on the map.

Not that that was a good thing. She certainly didn't want to be on any maps.

She crossed the street and turned down a quiet road that would lead her the back way home. She didn't want anyone to see her walking alone. Just then, a pair of headlights shone down the dark path, an engine revving. She turned around, staring at the truck.

Alex. She bit her tongue. What the hell did he want? Was he following her?

He sped up, squealing his tires next to her. "Get in," he called, staring down at her.

"What?"

"Get in. I'll take you home."

"Why would I do that?"

"Because it's the middle of the damn night, Gia. You don't need to be walking around dark alleys at night, alone."

"This is a street, not an alley."

"Still. Don't be difficult. Just get in the truck."

"No, thank you."

"Gia," he said, his voice raised. "Just get in the truck."

She stared at him. Was she supposed to be afraid of his stern voice? She wanted to tell him she dealt with so much worse at home. That there was no way he could destroy her when the worst monster of all was the one who had tucked her in to bed at night for years. Instead, she shook her head. "Why do you care, Alex?"

"Because, believe it or not, I care about you."

"I choose not."

He groaned. "Just let me take you home. You don't even have to talk to me. Daniel told me you were walking alone. I don't like it."

"Lucky for you, you don't have to like it." She began to walk again.

"I'm going to follow you. Even if you don't get in, I'm going to follow you and make sure you get home safely."

She turned around, rolling her eyes. "Oh my god, seriously?"

"Swear to god."

She huffed. "Fine. Whatever."

He stopped the truck, waiting as she walked around to the passenger's side. She opened the door, climbing in and buckling her seat belt, staring out the window with her arms crossed.

"Just home?" he asked. "Nowhere else you need to go?"

"Just home."

He sighed, stepping on the gas so the engine revved as he sped down the quiet street. Gia wouldn't look his way. She had no interest in talking to him, still fuming that he'd forced her hand.

He turned off the street that they'd been on, turning the opposite way of her house. "What are you doing?" she asked, her skin immediately going cold.

He smirked, his hands tight on the steering wheel. "Just a bit of a detour."

She clutched her stomach, staring at him. "What are you talking about? I want to go home."

He shook his head, rounding a curve a bit too sharply. "Oh, you'll be going home, Gia, don't worry about that. We just have to make a, erm, a pitstop first."

She swallowed, hearing the edge to his voice. "What are you doing, Alex? Please just let me out of the truck."

"Sorry, can't do that."

"What are you talking about? What's going on?" She was nervous, terrified honestly, and she hated it. She was so rarely scared. At least not like this. She didn't know what Alex was capable of, but she recognized that look in his eyes. The look of power. The look that told her he was in control and she was helpless. The look that Misty so often carried.

She bit her lip, feeling cool tears in her eyes. "Please tell me what's going on." He slowed down in front of Smoot Park, pulling into the dark parking lot. "What are we doing here?" she asked, her hand on the door handle.

He hit the automatic unlocking button, and she pulled the handle, prying the door open. She was planning to dart for it, but she stopped short. There were other cars waiting for them. Two more.

She watched Daniel step out of his car, three more guys with their hoods up following behind him. "What is this?" she asked, her voice so quiet she almost hadn't heard it herself.

Alex climbed out of the truck. "Rumors can only stay rumors for so long, Gia." He slammed the door shut, and she pushed the lock button, realizing what he was saying. The teens surrounded the truck, all five of them staring at her with evil grins. Daniel rubbed his hands together as if he were about to eat a delicious meal. As if she were the main course.

She scooted to the middle seat, knowing the truck wouldn't provide the solace she so desperately needed. They didn't move for her right away, choosing to stand and watch her panicking instead. She recognized the other boys' faces as they grew closer, besides Daniel and Alex, there was Isaac Bishop, Nathan Matthews, and Mitchell Evans. Boys that had graduated with Alex. Boys she only knew from passing in the hallway. Boys who had never looked twice at her until now. What had Alex told them? What did they want with her?

She heard the sharp click that let her know Alex was unlocking the doors and froze. She closed her eyes, cool tears forming once again, and prayed that this was all some horrible nightmare. That whatever they were planning, it was just a prank. That the hunger in their eyes was all in her imagination.

But she knew that wasn't the case. Alex reached into the truck, grabbing hold of her arm and pulling her to him. He looked down, not making eye contact with her. "Come on."

She whimpered, not moving. "Come on, Gia," he said more firmly. "Don't make this more difficult than it has to be."

He pulled her harder, grabbing hold of her leg, and with one final jerk she was out of the truck. He stood her on the ground, one hand on her shoulder.

"You don't have to do this," she said, trying to make eye contact with him. She wanted to beg, to plead for them to let her go, but she knew it was no use. It was obvious this had all been planned. They weren't going to let her go. She looked around the group, watching their faces, studying them.

Finally, Daniel spoke. "All right, let's get this over with."

Alex shoved her forward, pushing her through the parking lot and onto the wood chip-lined playground. She didn't speak anymore. She couldn't. Her lips were chattering, her whole body shaking with fear and adrenaline. She looked around, trying to decide if she could run, but there was no way. She was surrounded on every side, and the boys all towered over her, outweighing her by at least fifty pounds each.

The quiet night seemed so peaceful, though the storm raged in her as they came to a set of playground equipment. It hit her then, what they were going to do, and that they were actually going to do it. Knowing it would do no good, she used her elbow to shove Alex out of the way, catching them off guard as she began to run. Her feet slid through the wood chips but she kept her balance, headed for the road. Within seconds, a hand grabbed her hair, pulling her backwards. She let out a yelp, her voice bellowing through the night. "Please, stop! No!" she screamed louder, throwing fists and elbows in every direction, hoping and praying that someone would hear her. Someone who might care. A hand went over her mouth in an instant, Alex lifting her up and walking back to the slide.

"Don't make us hurt you," Daniel warned, his voice a low growl. Isaac lowered his hood as the boys grew closer.

"Isn't that what you're going to do anyway?" she asked, surprised by her own question.

"It doesn't have to be bad," Nathan said. "Some of them like it."

"Them?"

"Shut up," Alex warned him, pushing her down onto the black metal stairs. With two bounding steps, Nathan and Isaac climbed up the slide, towering above her. Alex and Daniel were behind her, with Mitchell to her right. They were staring at her, perhaps figuring out a game plan, as Alex began to lift her t-shirt. She was shaking, her body practically convulsing as he continued to undress her, several hands suddenly on her. Someone was stroking her hair as another unzipped her pants. She closed her eyes, feeling them being tugged from her hips. Alex grabbed hold of her, turning her over so her face was shoved into the metal.

"Give me her mouth," someone said. She knew the voice, but she couldn't be bothered to try and recognize it. Did it *even matter? She felt someone grab a wad of her hair, pulling it back so her face was lifted up. There were fingers in her mouth. Pants unzipping. More zippers. More hands. Tears fell from her eyes, and she sobbed and gagged as someone shoved themself into her mouth.*

Then someone else was shoving into her from behind. She tensed, and it hurt worse. Her pants were around her ankles, and she was naked from there up, completely exposed in a playground she'd played in so freely as a kid. Just a few feet away, she and Gavin had written their initials in permanent marker not so many years ago.

She tried to focus on that, on anything but the nightmare that was unfolding. Her mind grew fuzzy, allowing her to not think at all. This was something she was used to. The zoning out. The pretending to be somewhere else while the pain was inflicted. This was a different kind of abuse, sure, but was it any worse? She didn't know. She didn't want to know. It would be over soon, she promised herself. Just breathe.

So, she did. Breathing and surviving one moment at a time as her hip bones shoved into the metal of the stairs, her elbows growing raw from the rough texture of the coating. It was designed that way to keep kids from slipping, she knew. To keep them from getting hurt.

How ironic that this should be the place that would hurt her the most. When they were finished, the boys left, tossing her clothes at her without a word. Alex mumbled something about telling Gunner they said hello, but Gia couldn't focus. She just wanted them gone. She pulled her shirt over her head quickly, watching as the three vehicles left the dark park. She sank into the wood chips, heaving a sigh of relief as she took her first true breath since she'd left the party. Tears and snot poured down her cheeks as she rocked back and forth with silent sobs. Her chest was tight, her body sore, and she felt strangely numb. She couldn't process it. Or, perhaps, this was processing. She couldn't be sure.

She sat there, alone in the darkness, for most of the night, staring off into space in silence at times, allowing herself to be consumed by sobs at others. A few cars drove past the quiet park on occasion, but no one stopped to notice her. For that, she was incredibly grateful.

As the sun began to rise the next morning, she stood up, wrapping her arms around herself tightly and heading for home. She would have to make it home in time to cook breakfast, otherwise Misty would be furious.

She tried to decide what she should do. Who she should tell, could tell, about what had happened, but nothing made any sense in her mind. She could tell Gunner and Gavin, who might go after the guys and get themselves into trouble. She could tell Holly, who might feel sorry for her, but might also believe the rumors about her and Alex and therefore might not believe that this wasn't consensual. And, in the end, that's what it came down to. The rumors Alex had spread were what would hurt her chances of having anyone believe her. She could go to the doctor, tell the police what they'd done, but aside from Nathan, the boys all came from prominent families. Who was going to believe what she said over them? She didn't have the money for a lawyer, anyway. She could go to her grandmother, the only parent figure she'd ever known, but they hadn't spoken in years. Who was to say she'd even believe her? And if she did? What could she do about it? What could anyone do about it?

She took a breath, refusing to let herself cry again. She

wouldn't feel helpless. She wouldn't allow herself to feel like a victim. No. She was going to forget it had ever happened. The boys had graduated. It was so unlikely she'd ever have to see them again, anyway.

She'd lock up this night in the vault of her mind, another secret to tuck away. She already had so many, in the end, what was one more?

FIFTEEN

FIONA

Fiona and Logan had danced for most of the night, Fiona finally allowing herself to let just a bit of her guard down for the sake of Logan's happiness. Again, she wasn't sure why she cared. She shouldn't. She owed him nothing. And yet, she did. Undeniable. Irrefutable. She cared about Logan in a way she hadn't cared about someone for most of her life. All of her life, unless Gavin and Gunner counted.

But she hardly knew him. It was stupid. Foolish. She was asking to get her heart broken. When the night was over, they walked back to the hotel room, her feet burning from the heels. He shut the door behind her, staring at her with a warm expression.

"I had a lot of fun tonight," he said, his eyes dancing between hers.

"Me, too."

He leaned in slowly, kissing just beside of her mouth,

enough to make her heart skip a beat in her chest. "Thank you."

"For what?" she asked.

"For going with me. For not giving me too much trouble." His lips parted again as he moved his hand to cup her cheek. "For allowing me one night to forget about everything else."

She nodded. "Anytime."

"I want to kiss you again so badly," he said, his lips already moving toward hers.

"We shouldn't," she whispered, though her lips welcomed his before she could think of a reason why that was. His kiss was gentle, his mouth soft on hers. And, like the first kiss, it ended too soon.

"You're right," he said as he moved his lips to her nose and then her forehead. "We shouldn't. But, I'd never forgive myself if I didn't. Especially since we're going to be saying goodbye."

She took a step back, his words hitting her hard as she processed them. "What? What do you mean 'goodbye'?"

He walked past her, toward the beds, and began slipping out of his suit jacket, rolling up the sleeves of his shirt and slipping his tie off. "I mean, this is as far as I'm going with you. Tomorrow, when you leave, I won't be coming with you."

"What are you talking about? Why?"

"Because this is as far as I need to go," he said, unbuttoning the top buttons of his shirt so she had a view of his chest. Her throat went dry as she forced herself to look away.

"Did I do something wrong?"

"No," he said, stepping toward her. "Of course not." His voice was incredibly serious. "It has nothing to do with you."

She nodded, hating how much this news affected her. "Okay." She turned, walking toward the desk and kicking off her heels. She pulled her hair to the side. "Can you unzip me?" Was she trying to seduce him? To be honest, she wasn't entirely sure.

He swallowed, his eyes darting from hers to her dress and back again as she stared at him in the mirror. "S-sure," he said, his confidence suddenly seeming to have disappeared. He walked up behind her cautiously, his hands moving to her shoulders. Her breathing was slow as she watched him staring at her zipper. He brushed the rest of her hair over her shoulder, his eyes locking with hers in the mirror as he lowered his mouth to her neck. It was just a peck but her body was suddenly on fire. His fingers lowered the zipper, allowing her skin to be exposed to the cool air of the room. They stood, staring at each other, both waiting for the other to make a move. Finally, he ran a finger down her back, his lips parted, eyes filled with questions. She knew he must see her scars—the ones Misty had branded her with, the ones she hated to look at, and yet, he made no comment about them. Instead, he slipped the straps of her dress off her shoulders one at a time, his lips landing where the material had been. His tongue grazed her skin, and she let out a moan she hadn't been expecting.

That seemed to excite him. He moved the dress down over her hips slowly, his hands exploring her skin and leading the way for his mouth to follow. He kissed along her spine, his breath warming her skin. Finally, the dress fell to the floor, and she stood exposed in front of him except for her panties. Her face flushed, but she didn't move as he began to unbutton his shirt the rest of the way, pulling it from his arms quickly. He took hold of the back of her neck, spinning her around to him and pulling her into a kiss. Their lips met with passion this time, this kiss nothing like the ones they'd shared before. His tongue was entangling with hers, his fingers locked in her hair as he pulled her away from the desk. They moved throughout the room slowly, their lips never parting, though his hands did leave her hair to clutch her hips, guiding her toward the bed.

He took her hands, lacing his fingers through hers as he slid her down onto the bed, his body on top of hers. Their lips broke apart then, his eyes meeting hers, their breathing heavy. He nodded. "Wow."

She smiled. "Yeah."

He leaned down, biting her bottom lip gently. He kissed her chin, her jaw, her neck, lingering there for a bit as she squirmed with pleasure underneath him, then her collarbone, his tongue tracing a thin line down to her breasts. He cupped them carefully, running his thumb in circles over them. Her heart was going wild in her chest, her body pulsing under his touch. The man knew what he was doing, she had to give him that. Every part of her craved him, his skin sending lightning through hers.

Much to her disapproval, he released her breasts, moving to kiss her ribs, trailing his kisses down to her belly button and stopping at her panty line. He ran a finger over the forest-green cotton carefully, raising an eyebrow at her. She wasn't sure if it was a question, but she nodded just in case. He put his mouth to the fabric, running his tongue across her. His breath was warm through the material, and she lifted her hips, not wanting him to stop. He slid his fingers under the cotton, tugging at the panties, but she stopped him suddenly. "Could we turn off the light?" she asked.

He cocked his head to the side. "Why?"

She bit her lip, her face still flushed, but she couldn't seem to find an answer. He leaned back over top of her, kissing her lips carefully. "I want to see you, Fiona," he whispered, his words causing her insides to twist. "I want to see every inch of you." His hands were between her legs, his fingers causing her to let out a sigh of agreement.

He stood up, unbuttoning his pants and kicking off his shoes. He pulled his pants down slowly, almost strip-teasing her as he went. His eyes remained confident as he took off his boxers, never looking away or blushing. She couldn't keep her eyes from wandering as he stood in front of her, and he smirked as she did it, lowering himself to his knees in front of her and kissing the insides of her thighs as he pulled her panties off. She tried to retain the confident look she certainly didn't feel, and hoped it worked. He kissed between her legs, his tongue teasing her carefully, before standing up and attempting to flip her over onto her belly.

She froze, her body tightening without conscious thought. He stopped, letting go of her hips. "What's wrong?" She felt tears in her eyes again, suddenly embarrassed. It was as if she was reliving the night all over again, the shame filling her. "What is it?" he asked in horror. "Did I do something wrong?"

She shook her head, sitting up, crossing an arm over her chest in an attempt to cover herself. How pathetic was she? Crying over something that had happened nearly a decade ago.

"Talk to me, Fiona. Please," he said, touching her shoulder. He seemed to be unaware that they were still completely naked.

"I just...I can't...I can't *do it* like that."

"From behind?" he asked, his face serious.

She shook her head.

"Okay." He stroked her cheek. "I'm sorry if I upset you."

She nodded. "I'm sorry. This is ridiculous. You would think after all this time..." She stopped, rubbing a tear from her eyes. "I'm sorry. I ruined this." She stood up, walking to the head of the bed and covering up. He shook his head, standing up but making no move to cover up. He walked toward her.

"Do you not want this?"

Her bottom lip trembled. "No, it's not that. I do." She stared at him. "I really, really do. It's just..." She looked away.

"Just what?"

"You're going to think I'm stupid. Can we just forget about it?"

He lifted the covers, sliding in beside her, though still respectful of her space. "I won't think you're stupid, Fiona. You can talk to me. I've told you that."

She tried to kiss him, desperate to change the subject. "I really don't want to talk right now."

He kissed her, though his lips remained tight, and he ended the moment quickly. "I think you need to."

She sighed, staring up at the ceiling in an attempt to keep the tears at bay. "When I was seventeen, I was gang-raped by a bunch of boys I went to school with." She refused to look at him, though she could see the shock on his expression in her periphery. "It's not a big deal. It was a long time ago, and I'm over it. I don't want to talk about it, but I just...I can't...that was how he, *they,* I mean...I just..." Tears were staring to pour then, and Logan touched her chin, pulling her face down so that their eyes met.

"It's okay," he said firmly. "I get it."

She nodded, not wanting to acknowledge how vulnerable she felt. "I'm sorry. I know this is completely ruining everything."

He wrapped an arm around her, pulling her into a hug. "Fiona, you aren't ruining anything. I'm glad you're talking to me. I'm glad you're being honest with me. I'm so...I'm so sorry that happened to you."

She nodded. "Thank you." She cleared her throat, wiping away a tear quickly. "I had always pictured this moment...wondered if it would happen, you know, I mean, oh god, that sounded stupid. I just...I never knew how I would feel. Or how many memories it would bring up for me. I mean, you were great, what you were doing...it felt good, I wasn't thinking about them, I just—" She groaned, covering her face with her palms. "Can you just put me out of my misery, please?"

He pulled her hands away carefully, his expression calm. "Are you saying...am I the first person you've been with since then?"

"The first person I've wanted to be with." She nodded, biting her lip. "I've had sex since then...but never because I wanted to. Only when it was what I had to do to survive."

"You mean for money?"

She lifted her head in a small nod, avoiding his eyes. "Yeah, sometimes. But, it was always cold. I wasn't thinking about anything with them. This is...this felt different. Real, I guess." She looked at him. "I'm just not sure what to expect. My romantic life has been somewhat...uneventful."

He closed his eyes, leaning his head back. "I'm so sorry."

"Don't be sorry," she said. "I'm fine, honestly. It was forever ago. I just need to...stay on my back, maybe? I don't know. I can keep you posted." She tried to laugh. "God, who am I kidding? You probably think I'm insane. What kind of person would be crazy enough to sleep with me? I basically just told you I was a prostitute. I can't even shut—"

He kissed her lips, ending her sentence, his hand cupping her cheek again. When he pulled away, he spoke slowly. "I want to be very clear, Fiona. I am the kind of person crazy enough to sleep with you. I am. I think you're...you're beautiful and strong and sexy as hell. And, I want to do things to you that will keep this entire hotel awake all night." He paused, her insides warming back up at his words. How on earth did he get to be so confident? And what was it about his confidence that made him so irresistible? "I don't care what you've done in the past. But I need you to talk to me. I need you to tell me what works for you and what doesn't. If you feel uncomfortable, I want to know. If something I do, god, if anything I do doesn't make you feel safe or good or, hell, whatever. If you aren't turned on by my every move, I want you to tell me." He nodded. "Deal?"

Her lips were parted as she answered. "Deal."

"I'm going to go slow," he said. "So slow I'm going to drive you mad." He kissed her jaw in slow motion as if to prove a point. "But this night, I'm going to make sure this night is one you're going to remember for the rest of your life." He kissed her collar bone. "I'm going to show you how good sex can be, Fiona, and I'm going to make sure that tomorrow when we say goodbye...well, I'm going to make sure it's not the last time you'll think of me."

He slid back on top of her before she could answer, his lips meeting hers again, his kisses slow, his hands meticulous. He was right already, she knew. Even if they didn't have sex, even if the entire night ended right then, she knew there was no way she'd forget him anytime soon. How could she forget the only eyes who'd ever looked at her like he did? Like she wasn't the monster she could never tell him she was.

She closed her eyes, allowing herself to sink further into his kiss as their bodies began moving together. He slid a hand between her legs again, his lips on her ear. "No rush," he whispered as her head went back in pleasure from his touch. "We have all night. And I plan to use every minute of it."

God, she prayed that was true.

SIXTEEN

FIONA

Somewhere in the distance, there was a distinct buzzing noise. Fiona rolled over, Logan's arm sliding off of her, though he did not wake. She sat up, holding the covers so that it covered her bare chest as she stared around the room. She rubbed her sleep-coated eyes with her free hand, wondering where the noise could be coming from and what it might be.

Finally, she stood up, taking the comforter with her as she walked around the room, searching for the disturbance. She had one eye closed as she looked around. For a moment, the noise stopped and she wondered if she had dreamed it. Just as soon as she began to walk back to the bed, it began again. This time, more awake, she realized it was a phone vibrating.

Curious, she walked toward Logan's bag with one look over her shoulder to make sure he was still sound asleep.

Though he'd been somewhat reserved about his life in general, his backpack was one thing he hadn't spoken of at all. He wouldn't let her come near it and never opened it or took anything from it when she was around. One thing she knew for sure, was that he'd mentioned several times that he had no cell phone. So, then, what was vibrating from his bag?

She'd been so caught up in keeping her own secrets, she'd never taken the time to try and find his. She opened the main compartment, the zipper extra loud in the quiet room. She checked on Logan again, letting out a breath as she was reassured he was still asleep. She sifted through the bag, a few changes of clothes, a toothbrush, his wallet. Finally, she saw a dim light at the bottom of his bag and shoved her hand further in, reaching for it.

She pulled the small flip-phone from the depths of his bag, staring at the small square screen that held two letters, **FD**, and then a phone number she didn't recognize. Her initials. What were the chances? It felt too big to be a coincidence. She considered not answering it, knowing that she probably shouldn't, but she was curious. She flipped open the phone, immediately regretting the decision as Logan stirred in his sleep. She held the phone to her ear, not wanting to make a sound to wake him.

And then she heard the words that caused her heart to plummet.

"How is she?"

SEVENTEEN

LOGAN

THREE MONTHS AGO

"Serena," he said, looking up to greet her as she walked into his office. "Good morning."

She smiled at him, running a hand through her frazzled hair. "Good morning."

He stood up from his chair, approaching her. "How are you feeling? I didn't realize you'd be coming in today."

She nodded. "I scheduled the appointment last minute. I assumed Madeline would've told you."

"Is everything all right?"

"No," she said, shaking her head as her jaw began to quiver. "No, nothing's all right." Her eyes began to fill with tears and his throat went dry.

"What is it, sweetheart?" he asked, touching her shoulders carefully.

"I have something to tell you," she said softly.

"Okay, go on then," he said, sitting down and patting the seat in front of him for her to sit as well. She turned, walking away from him, her hands twisting together in front of her. "You're scaring me," he said, trying to laugh.

She turned back around. "I'm so sorry, Logan."

"Well, you don't have to be sorry, just tell me what's going—"

"I've lied to you. I've been lying to you. About everything." She spit the words out, her eyes closed.

"What?" he asked, his jaw dropping open as the words slammed into his chest. "What are you talking about?"

She shook her head. "I never meant for any of this to happen. Honestly, I didn't. I came to you for help. I never thought that I would...that I would fall in love with my therapist. I mean, these things don't just happen. I never expected—"

"Serena, what are you saying?"

She stopped pacing then, looking him in the eye, her expression filled with anguish. "I'm married."

If he hadn't already been sitting, he would've been then. "You're...you're what?" He looked away, unsure of how to process the devastation and betrayal he felt.

"I'm married," she said, grimacing. "I'm so sorry."

"You're...married?"

"I'm so sorry," she whispered again. "I don't know why I didn't tell you before. I wanted to. I thought about it so many times, but I just couldn't. I didn't want to hurt you."

He stood up, walking away from her and toward the window. He couldn't find the words to say what he was thinking, nor the thoughts to think what he was feeling. He pressed his head onto the warm glass of the window, closing his eyes.

Finally, he spoke the only words he could possibly muster. "We have to stop seeing each other." He swallowed. "I can recommend another doctor for you."

"Don't you want to talk about this? I'm only telling you now because I think I want to tell my husband about us. I'm choosing you. I want to choose you."

"Don't do that," he told her. "Please just don't. I would've never...if I'd known..." He spoke over his shoulder. "I will find you another doctor. Someone who can help you. I'm sorry, Serena, I can't see you anymore. This isn't right."

She whimpered. "I don't want another doctor, Logan. I want you. I've always wanted you. You saved my life when no one else could."

"I also broke every code of ethics there is the moment that I let our relationship become anything but professional." He turned back around to her. "I'm sorry. This isn't your fault. You're sick. I took advantage of that."

"No," she cried, tears pouring down her cheeks. "No, you didn't. This is my fault. I should have told you the truth, it's just that by the time I realized I was falling for you, it was too late."

"It doesn't matter, Serena. I should've never let it happen. That was my job. To protect you—"

"You did—"

"I didn't. I knew better. I'm not a rule breaker. I should've never allowed the line to be crossed." He sucked in a breath. "No matter how badly I wanted it to." She took a step toward him, but he stepped back. "You need to go, Serena. I'll have one of my colleagues call you and get you on their calendar." He felt cool tears lining his eyes and turned away,

not able to watch her cry any longer. "I'm so sorry I let this happen."

"But, I love you," she said, her voice full of desperation. "I can't just let the past year come to an end like this. I love you. I want to be with you."

He shook his head, still not looking at her. "You need to go, Serena. I can't do this anymore. You should go be with your husband."

"I thought we were going to get a divorce," she said, her voice closer to him than he'd expected. "When I came to you, I was planning to leave him. He didn't care about my depression. Not enough to do anything more than write a check. You cared. You took care of me."

He spun around. "Because it was my job." Anger filled him then, anger he hadn't meant to allow himself to feel. "But falling in love with you wasn't my job. Loving you isn't my job. That's your husband's. So, if you are still married to him, you need to leave. You need to go be with him. I'm sorry. I have to go." He stormed out of the office, fresh tears in his eyes, and hurried past his worried-looking secretary without a word. How had he let himself get so screwed up?

A WEEK LATER, *on his first day back at the office, Madeline popped her head into his door. "Good to see you back," she said, offering him a bright smile.*

"Thanks, Madeline. It's good to be back." He wasn't lying. Though he had needed the break, a bit of fresh air to clear his mind, Logan couldn't deny how much he'd missed

his practice—how much he missed being able to help his patients.

"Um, I don't know if this is the best time, but while you were away, you had a new patient request." She looked down, stepping further into his office and shutting the door. "He was, erm, rather persistent. I tried to explain to him that you aren't open to new patients right now, but he seemed really upset. He said you're the only one he could see. He's been calling every day."

"Did you offer to let him see Mel? She's got several openings."

"I did," she said. "He insisted on seeing you. I can put him on the waitlist if you want, I just...I wasn't sure what to do."

"Clear out my lunch," he said finally, letting out a sigh. "I'll see him today for a consult and try to talk him into seeing Mel or Steve."

She nodded. "Okay, I'll let him know. Do you need anything else?"

"No," he said. "Thanks though."

WHEN IT CAME *time for the new patient to arrive, Logan was already back into the groove of his usual workday. He was exhausted from having to explain to Aaron that he wasn't dying, no matter how many times he'd WedMD'd his symptoms; he was heartbroken from watching Noelle cry on his couch over her husband's death. He'd held Donna's hand as she recalled her traumatic childhood and given candy to a young girl named Ashleigh as she talked about her grandmother's death. His job, though not physically taxing usually, was mentally and emotionally exhausting. It drained and exhilarated him in a way that he both loved and hated.*

As the door opened, a man with buzz cut brown hair and red, puffy eyes walked in. He had a thick jacket on despite the warm weather, and his bloodshot eyes locked on Logan the second he entered the room.

Grief. Logan recognized it immediately. "Hi," he said, standing up and shaking the man's hand. "I'm Logan. It's nice to meet you."

"I'm Tom. Tom Stephenson." The name hit Logan, causing him to swallow. "I know you're trying to decide if that means I'm who you think I am," he said, before Logan could respond. "And it does."

Logan stared at him, his mouth opening and closing as he tried to decide what to say. "You're Serena's..."

"Husband," he confirmed. "Yes. So then, you did know about me."

Logan grabbed hold of the chair behind him, trying to maintain composure. He took a breath. "I'm...I'm sorry." He watched the man's eyes fill with tears again. "I'm so terribly sorry."

Tom's lips began quivering, a fat tear on his eyelid. "Did you love her?" he asked, his lips hardly moving, face growing red.

"I didn't know she was married."

"But you knew she was your patient," he said, touching his temple. "You knew she was your sick, suicidal patient who came to you for help after we lost our child."

"I know." He lowered his shoulders. "I should've never crossed the line. I'm so sorry. There's no amount of words that could possibly make this okay. I realize that. I've asked Serena

not to come back. I won't see her anymore. Not ever. I promise you. If I had known about your marriage, I would've never..."

"I know," the man said. "You don't have to worry about seeing her ever again." Tears spilled down his cheeks as he bent over his knees, sobs tearing him apart. Logan leaned forward, trying to reach out to him, but the man stood up defensively. He pulled a gun from his jacket pocket, pointing it directly at Logan.

"Woah!" Logan shouted, ice-cold fear filling him instantly. "What are you doing?" He held his hands up, moving out of the way of the weapon, but it followed him.

"You were supposed to help her, man." He wiped his cheek with the sleeve of his jacket, his voice no longer sad but rather, filled with anger. "You were supposed to help her, and instead you're the reason she's gone. I loved her more than anything. And you took her from me. You took her from me in every way there was to take her."

Logan blinked rapidly, looking around the room in a desperate attempt to understand what Tom was telling him. "She's dead?"

"Yeah, didn't you hear me? She killed herself two days ago. Because of you. Because she fell in love with someone who didn't love her back. All the while, I loved her more than anything and she could never see that. Never. I sent her to you because I trusted you to help her."

Logan closed his eyes, his throat dry. "I don't know what to say, Tom. I had no idea—"

"What? You had no idea that she was sick?"

"No, of course I did, I just—"

"You had no idea that she was coming to you because she

was grieving the loss of our daughter and that she might be confused and vulnerable—"

"It wasn't like that. I didn't—"

He shoved the gun closer to him. "You didn't what? You didn't take advantage of her? You didn't effectively kill her yourself?"

Logan didn't move, the words destroying what little resolve he had left. Tears filled his eyes. He'd been trained on how to handle people like this. He knew what he should do to calm him down, but at the moment, nothing seemed like it would work. His brain wasn't computing what needed to be done, it was filled with too much shock. "I cared about her." He met the man's eyes. "It's no excuse. It doesn't make it okay, but it's the truth. I did. I cared about her very much. And I'm so very sorry for your loss. But, you need to put the gun down. It's not going to help anything. I know you're upset. I know you're angry and hurt, and I know the person you want to take that all out on right now is me, but I'm asking you to take a breath. Serena wouldn't have wanted—"

"Don't try to shrink me, man. You don't know me. You don't know the first thing about me or my wife. You just...you took advantage of her. She'll never mean to you what she meant to me."

He nodded. "I know that. She couldn't. She's your wife. She loved you."

"Not enough to stay." With that, he fired. The deafening sound tore through the office, and Logan ducked, though the bullet wasn't close to him. Screams could be heard throughout the building as people began running through the usually empty halls.

He heard Madeline's voice. "I think it was Logan!"

"Just go!" Mel shouted.

The shot seemed to catch Tom off guard, and he looked around, though his eyes narrowed again, firing in Logan's direction once more. He picked up the leather chair, chucking it at his attacker. Tom ducked as the chair slammed into the wall. Logan darted behind the couch just as Tom fired again, this time the bullet tore through the couch, ripping into Logan's shoulder at lightning speed. He covered his collar bone, screaming out. The pain ripped through him, radiating in waves of tremendous pain. Tom was heading toward him again, and Logan pushed himself up, running toward the door. Another shot, two more. One connected with his calf, burning as it burrowed into his muscle. He pulled open the door, hobbling out and knowing this would be it for him. He was going to die. There was no way around it. The blood soaked through his palms, as he desperately tried to staunch the bleeding. He heard the footsteps, knew Tom was coming for him, and made one final attempt to save himself. He hurried to the elevator, pushing the button and wiggling in place as he waited for the door to open.

"You don't just get to run away from this," Tom's bellowing voice called. "She's dead because of you. You don't get to live."

Logan turned his head to look at him just as he fired a shot. Behind him, the elevator door opened, and Logan heard a thud. He spun around in time to see Madeline sliding to the floor, a bullet hole in her forehead. He gasped, looking back at Tom, who also looked visibly surprised.

"What did you do?" he demanded, hurrying into the elevator and pressing the button to close the door.

"No," Tom said, raising his gun. "I may have pulled the

trigger, but you loaded the gun. So, the question is, what did you do?"

The elevator doors closed as he fired again and again. He fell to the floor, watching as the bullets ripped through the doors without a problem. Logan stared at Madeline's crumpled body on the floor, a large knot in his chest. Tom was right. What had he done?

EIGHTEEN

FIONA

Fiona stared at the phone, her hands shaking. It was a number she didn't recognize. She waited for him to speak again.

"Logan?" the man asked.

She took a sharp breath. "Who is this?" she demanded, keeping her voice low.

With that, the line clicked and she was left in silence. She thought quickly, realizing she'd been played. Logan was after her. He'd come to hurt her. She set his phone down, walking to her bag and pulling out the knife she'd used to kill Danielle. She pulled the dress over her head quickly, staring at him. Her senses were on high alert, her skin tingling as she watched his chest rising and falling. She didn't want to kill him. That was never her plan. But now she had to. Once again, her hand was forced. It was her or him. And she'd choose herself every time.

She flicked on the overhead light, causing him to stir. He rubbed his eyes, sitting up, his eyes widening as he saw the knife she held pointed at him.

"Who are you?" she asked through bared teeth.

He shook his head, putting his hands up. "What are you talking about?"

"Don't play dumb with me, Logan. Who the fuck are you, and who sent you?"

He stood up from the bed, moving toward her. She stepped back, the knife held firmly in her hands between them. "Fiona, what are you talking about?"

"I answered your phone. You know, the phone you don't have? It was ringing. And when I answered, someone asked how *she* was. I'm gonna assume *she* is me."

His face went ashen, and he touched his mouth. "Fiona, I—"

"I thought you liked me—god, I was so stupid. I should've never *never* trusted you."

"Do you?" He raised an eyebrow. "Do you trust me?"

"What?"

"Do you? You said you should've never trusted me, but that knife tells me you never did." He stepped closer.

"I will kill you," she said. "If you thought you could trick me or use me or whatever the hell this is, you're wrong. I will kill you. And I won't think twice about it."

"Because you've done it before?"

She swallowed. "What did you say?"

"You've...you've killed before, huh?"

"You don't know anything about me."

"I know that you mean it when you say you're going to kill me. Just like I know that's a choice you've had to make before. I can see how comfortable you are with the decision. I can see that your eyes have already shut down, you're closing off to me. You aren't allowing yourself to feel."

"What are you talking about, Logan?"

He sighed, putting a hand up to shield himself from the knife that was moving closer to him. "I didn't want to tell you like this. I didn't want to...I don't know." He rubbed a palm over his face, looking around the room. "I didn't want to lie to you, Fiona. I didn't lie to you. Not about everything."

"Not about everything?" She scoffed. "Just a few things, then? A lie is a lie, Logan. I don't care how many times you did it."

"It's not like that. I do care about you. Honestly, I do. I...there are things you should know about me, of course, but I didn't lie about that."

"So start talking," she said, pushing the knife forward quickly.

"Could you at least lower that thing?" He gestured down at his scantily clad body. "I'm hardly a threat to you right now."

Her eyes flickered down, and she lowered the knife slightly. "Sit down," she told him, kicking the chair beside her toward him. "Sit down now. Keep your hands where I can see them."

He sat down, chuckling to himself. "I'm not going to hurt you, Fiona."

"Yeah, well, I've heard that before." She sat down on the bed in front of him, her fingers still wrapped around the knife. "Now, who was on the phone?"

"In order for me to tell you that, I need to tell you about my past."

"I've asked you about your past before."

"I wasn't ready to talk about it then."

"But you are now?"

He bit his lip, brushing a piece of his curly hair from his face. "I don't really have a choice."

"There's always a choice, Logan. Your choice now is to talk or die."

He swallowed, his eyes growing wide. "Okay. Okay, so before we met, I was a doctor. A psychologist."

"A shrink? Do you work for the clinic? Did they send you to find me?"

"What? *No*. What clinic?"

She shook her head.

"Fiona, were you receiving psychiatric care before you met me?"

"This isn't about me," she said firmly. "Why aren't you a psychologist anymore? What does any of this have to do with me?"

Tears filled his eyes suddenly, and he pressed his fingers to his lips. He cleared his throat, looking away. When he spoke, his voice was soft. "I, um, I made a mistake. And someone, *multiple people*, died because of that mistake."

"What are you talking about? What mistake?"

"I fell in love," he said, clearing his throat again and adjusting in his chair. "I fell in love with Serena. The woman I told you about." He waited for her to nod in recognition before he went on. "She was...very, very off limits to me."

"Okay..." She waited for him to go on.

"She was my patient. A patient who came to me after she had lost a child." He looked away again, his eyes swimming with tears once more. "I was supposed to help her. And

I did, I guess. But, we had this connection. This incredible connection that I can't really explain. We...we fell in love. It wasn't one-sided, but she wasn't well. I knew better. I should've never allowed myself to accept my feelings for her. As a doctor, patients developed feelings for me all the time, for all doctors...it's a very natural thing. But, we aren't supposed to feel the same way. We aren't supposed to allow ourselves to get close to our patients even though we go so deep into their pasts and psyche that we literally know them better than they know themselves. It's...it's something I always struggled with." He shook his head. "But I'd never let myself cross the line. *Never.* Until I met her. She was...smart and funny. She could make me laugh. Oh, and sometimes I could make her laugh." He smiled, seeming to be remembering. "It was...*she* was perfect."

"So, what happened?"

"She told me she was married."

Fiona took a sharp breath.

"Yeah," Logan said, "so, of course, I broke it off immediately. I was trying to do the right thing in a situation I'd already screwed up so badly. But, it didn't matter. Serena was...she was broken. She had experienced so much loss by the time that I'd met her. I should've seen how badly she needed help. But, I didn't. I chose to believe I could fix her. That I *had* fixed her. That somehow me loving her was enough to make her depression go away. Enough to make her forget all the darkness." He wiped a stray tear from his cheek as quickly as it fell, looking back to Fiona then. "I had lost so many people, too. I guess it was why we connected so well."

"Who?" Fiona asked, though it didn't matter. She didn't care. Correction, she *shouldn't* care. And yet, she did.

"My parents." He sniffed. "And my younger brother." He closed his eyes. "It was my fault."

"Your fault?"

"I was in medical school—my parents both worked two jobs to put me through college. So, a lot of the responsibility that came with watching my brother fell on me. He was fourteen, so it wasn't like I had to do everything for him, but they expected me to be there, you know? Anyway, one night I had picked him up from school and hurried home. I had a big test to study for, and I was distracted. It's no excuse. None of this is any excuse. He was still my responsibility."

"What happened?"

"He, um, he snuck out with a few of his friends. He'd done it before. I was supposed to check on him, but I got busy and I forgot about it." He shook his head, looking down. When he looked back up, there were more tears in his eyes though his face was stony. "He never came home."

"I'm sorry," she said, feeling her fingers loosen on the knife a little.

"Drunk driver," he said. "He ran up onto the sidewalk. Killed four of them that night, including Damon. My parents never forgave me."

"It wasn't your fault."

"Yes it was. It's all my fault. A few years later, my mom passed away. Dad went shortly after. I never got to say goodbye. They wouldn't even talk to me." He lowered his head again. "God, I sound pathetic. I know you couldn't care less about this, but I'm telling you this so you understand why I did things the way I did. Why I fell in love with Serena. Why I'm falling in love with you."

She swallowed, standing up from the bed. Her head

shook involuntarily. "No." She grabbed her bag from the floor, pulling on her shoes. "No."

"Fiona, wait," he said, trying to reach for her.

She jerked her arm away quickly, grabbing her keys and shoving past him. "Don't fall in love with me, Logan. I'm not worth it."

"Fiona, please," he said, "please don't go like this."

"I have to." She pulled open the door, feeling the burn of tears in her eyes. "Don't follow me." When she felt him grabbing the door, though he was still dressed in only his boxer briefs, she spun back around, the knife in the air once more. "I said don't follow me."

He took a step back, his Adam's apple bobbing as he stared at the knife. "Okay."

She shut the door, hurrying toward the elevator. Her entire body shook. Why had she been foolish enough to let him in? Why had she allowed herself to feel anything for this man? To let him believe he could feel something for her, too? There was nothing about her that was worthy of love. And that story about his past? She couldn't handle anyone with that much heartache. She had enough of her own.

As the elevator doors opened, she rushed out of them, her shoes slapping the marble floor loudly. A few people stared at her as she rushed past, but no one dared try and stop her. She stuck the key into the car door, jiggling it to get it to unlock. Just as she did, she looked over. A man was approaching her, a buzz cut head and dark, shadowy eyes. In the dark parking lot, he seemed menacing.

"Hello, are you okay?" he asked, stopping a few feet from her.

"I'm fine," she said, pulling the door open and moving to climb inside.

"Are you staying here?"

"I'm not," she said. "Not anymore."

"*Fiona!*" Logan's voice called out to her from the lobby's doors. The man spun around.

"Well, well, well...we meet again."

"Get away from her!" Logan yelled, barging at her at top speed. Before Fiona could process what was happening, the man turned back to Fiona, a wicked grin on his face.

"An eye for an eye," he cackled, pulling a gun from his pocket. Her eyes connected with Logan for just a second, as he launched through the air toward the man. At the same time, the gun's blast could be heard and pain suddenly tore through her, white hot and fierce. She staggered back, a hand over her thigh as the blood began to pool out. She blinked rapidly, trying to remain conscious as she fell to the ground. She could hear the men grunting as they fought. Logan knocked the gun from his hand, and it launched to the ground, skidding across the pavement. She was intensely grateful her attacker no longer held it. But then she began to worry. What if the man won? What if he got the gun back? Would he kill Logan? Would he kill them both? Who was the man, after all? What did he mean by 'an eye for an eye'?

She reached her hand out, searching for the cool metal of the weapon, her fingers outstretched as far as they would go. She sighed, pulling herself up onto her elbows and scooting an inch closer. Finally, she connected with the gun, picking it up with a shaking, blood-covered hand. She pointed it in their direction, her vision growing blurry.

Her finger found the trigger as she watched them wrestle. If she pulled it, she would hit one of them. Potentially both of them. Was it a risk she was willing to take? She wished it was that simple. She'd always chosen herself, her own safety, over others. *Her or them.* But Logan's words kept echoing in her quiet mind. He was falling in love with her. Currently, he was trying to save her.

Who was this man, anyway? Was he the man from the phone? Was he after her? Knowing what she had to do, she adjusted her finger on the trigger. She had no choice.

Her finger moved, ready to pull, and then...it all went black.

NINETEEN

FIONA

White lights. Bright, white lights. They burned her eyes. Her nose, too. No, wait. What was that burning her nose? It was so cold. Air? It felt like air. She blinked again, moving a hand to shield her eyes. Something was blowing cool air straight to her nose.

She felt someone squeeze her other hand, and she looked in that direction. *Logan. The liar. The betrayer. The man who was in love with her.*

"What are you doing here?" she asked, her throat incredibly dry.

"Oh, thank god," he said, rubbing a piece of hair from her face. She realized then how bloodshot his eyes were. He'd been crying.

She glanced around the room, still slightly confused. "Where are we?"

"We're at the hospital." He pressed his lips together in a grimace. "I'm so sorry."

Suddenly, it began to come back to her. *The man. The gun. The pain.* She touched her thigh, running her fingers over the exposed gauze bandages. "Who was that man?"

He frowned. "His name is Tom," he said. "And he wanted me dead. I'm so sorry you got dragged into my mess."

"Why did Tom want you dead?" she asked, trying to readjust with a wince on her face.

"Serena was his wife," he said, his eyes locked on hers.

"Oh."

"After she told me she was married, I broke it off, just like I told you. A week later...she was dead."

"Oh," she repeated.

"I'm so sorry, Fiona. I'm so sorry for all of this. I...I was terrified. I didn't know what to do. He came to the place I worked and gunned me down. He tried to kill me and I was scared and so, I ran. I should've never gotten you involved. Hell, I should've never slept with a patient." He squinted his eyes. "Two women are dead because of me. Because of my actions. Serena is gone. My secretary, Madeline, was killed in the crossfire when Tom came to my office to kill me." He looked down. "You could've been the third. It should've been me. Only me. No one else should've died. I'm just so sorry. I don't know what I would've done if you'd died. I couldn't have handled it."

"You didn't mean for them to die," Fiona said. "It's not your fault." She wasn't saying it to make him feel better necessarily, but more because it was the truth.

"It's still my fault. It was my actions that caused it."

"Trust me. I've been in Tom's shoes." She swallowed,

unsure why she was admitting the truths she'd never told anyone. "I've killed. And no one's actions made me do it. It was my choice. Falling in love doesn't make you a criminal, getting someone pregnant doesn't mean you deserve to lose the only person you've ever loved."

Logan lowered his brow. "What?"

She shook her head. "Nothing." Why was she feeling so open? What pain meds were they giving her, anyway?

He reached up, taking her hand carefully. "You can tell me anything," he said softly. "I'm not going to leave you."

"Because you're falling in love with me?" she asked.

He nodded. "I don't say that to scare you off. I know you aren't the most open person. I know love must terrify you. I know my track record for falling in love isn't the greatest, but it's true. There's something about you, Fiona. Something dark. Something, a piece of you, that I connect to in some crazy way. It's like...you were what I've been looking for all this time."

She rolled her eyes. "You just like fixing people. You have a hero complex—an obsession with women you can heal."

He ran a thumb over her knuckles, not denying it. "It's who I am, Fiona. I won't apologize for that. I like helping people. My job means I see people at their worst and try to get them back to some semblance of normal. You are broken. But, that's not why I'm here right now. I'm here because somewhere inside of you is something good. Something that maybe you've forgotten even exists. I see that part of you. I want you to see it, too."

"There's nothing good about me."

"Because you're a killer?"

She nodded. "I've killed or lost everyone that ever mattered to me."

He flinched. "So, you've killed more than once?"

Again, she nodded, her lips tight.

"Tell me more."

"I...can't," she whispered. "It tears me apart to talk about it."

"Sometimes talking about it is exactly what you need."

"Thanks, doc."

He smirked. "I'm not asking as a doctor. I'm asking as a friend. As someone who hopes to someday be more."

"I'm telling you I'm a killer and you're asking me out?" She snorted. "Maybe you're the one who needs to see a shrink."

"It's those of us who are broken ourselves that can most connect to others like us." He stared at her intently, waiting for her to begin talking. Upon realizing she wasn't going to, he spoke again. "What if I guess? I'll let you know what I think I know and you can confirm."

She put a hand over her leg, where her pain was coming from, but nodded. "Okay."

"Okay," he said, seeming surprised by that answer. "Okay, well...you said you killed the girl someone got pregnant?"

She closed her eyes. "You aren't bothered by that?"

His thumb continued massaging her hand, his eyes filled with a calm understanding. He wasn't looking at her as though she were a monster. Instead, he was trying to understand. Trying to see her side of things. "I've heard worse."

She looked down, not denying it.

"Okay, so was it your boyfriend, then?" he asked. She

began to answer, though her voice caught in her throat. She couldn't talk about it. Couldn't bring him up. It was just too hard to think about Fle—"Was it Fletcher?"

Her eyes darted up to meet his. "What did you say?" She pulled her hand back from his. *FD...Fletcher Denali? Did Logan know Fletcher?*

"I, um, I...okay, please don't get mad. Someone at the hotel called the police after Tom shot you. Or maybe after I shot him, I don't know. Anyway, I needed the police to be able to help you, but I didn't want you to get into any trouble. So, I went through your bag." Her gaze flickered around the room, searching for the black bag. It was the only thing in the world, besides her car, that she owned. Her whole life was hidden in the contents of that bag. "I took your knife and your cash and stashed them for you. They're in the car. But, I also found a phone. A phone with one number saved into it. Fletcher's number. You'd called him several times but each time it was for only a few seconds. Hang-ups, I'm assuming. Those are usually the result of a broken heart. I know it's snooping, and it's not any of my business. But, I was scared. If something happened to you, I wanted to be able to tell someone. I wanted someone else to feel the loss like I was going to. You didn't deserve to die alone."

"Am I dying?" she asked, panic filling her at his words.

"No," he answered. "You're stable. But I couldn't possibly know that before."

"Fletcher wasn't my boyfriend."

He nodded. "Okay. So, who was he?"

She bit her lip. "It doesn't matter who he was. He's a stranger now. I'm never going to see him again. He hates me."

"Why would you say that?"

"Because it's true," she said firmly. "Because Fletcher is —" She stopped talking as the door opened, and she stared into a face that instantly brought tears to her eyes. "Fletcher is here."

TWENTY

FIONA

Fletcher walked into the room, his face ghost-white. "Fi?" he asked, his voice small.

"Fletcher? What are you doing here?" She tried to sit up but found it hurt too badly.

"I called him," Logan said, standing up. "I'm sorry, Fiona. I was terrified. I didn't know what to do. I called him and asked him to come."

"You shouldn't have done that."

"Yes," another voice said. She looked to the door where Gunner was walking in. "He should have."

"Gunner?"

He nodded. Fletcher pulled his sister into a hug. "I've been so worried about you." He rubbed the back of her head.

"I'm sorry," she told him when he stood back. "I'm so sorry about everything."

"What happened?" Gunner asked Logan.

"She...she got tangled up in my past," he answered. "She was shot by a man who wanted me dead. He's..." He cleared his throat. "He's dead now. He won't be hurting her anymore."

"He's dead?" Fiona asked, staring at Logan. "You killed for me?"

"I couldn't let him hurt you," he said simply.

"Who are you, anyway?" Fletcher demanded. Suddenly both men were staring Logan down.

"He's a friend," Fiona said defensively. She met Logan's eyes in between her brothers. "He's been taking care of me. And none of this is his fault."

"You shouldn't have left the clinic, Fiona. You were safe there."

"How did you get out anyway?"

"It doesn't matter. I am out."

Fletcher leaned down, cupping her face. "You have to go back, Fi. You need help."

"The only help I was getting there was from a doctor who screwed me twice a day," she bit her tongue, trying to keep the tears at bay, "in exchange for pills. I saved up enough to end my life. Three times. Three times, Fletcher. That place wasn't helping me. It was destroying me."

Fletcher's jaw grew tight. "Why didn't you tell me? I would've gotten you out of there."

"You never came to see me. You didn't write or call. You left me alone. And I can't say that I blame you. I killed Holly. I'm so sorry. I'm so sorry for all of it." She felt a sob burning her chest as Fletcher's expression grew sad.

"I came to visit every week, Fi. Every week. They wouldn't let me see you. They wouldn't let me contact you at all."

"They never told me that." She rubbed her eye. "They told me you weren't coming."

"I would never leave you alone. You know that. We're in this together, Fiona. We always have been."

"But, how could you ever forgive me?"

"How could I not?" he asked. "I hate you for what you did. Holly..." He paused, running a palm over his face and through his beard. "Holly should've lived. But, I know why you did it. You were always the brave one. The protector."

"I just wanted to save us all," she said. "There were too many secrets. There still are."

"And we just keep adding to them," Gunner said from behind Fletcher. He wasn't looking at her, but rather at Logan.

"Fiona, what did you do to Danielle?" Fletcher asked, looking at his brother.

"Who?"

"The note you left on my door," Gunner answered. "What did you do with her?"

Danielle Harris. She remembered the name from her ID, then. She covered her mouth. "I...I had to get rid of her. She was going to kill the girl you were with, Fletcher. I needed to protect you from any more loss."

"You can't just go around killing people, Gia," Gunner said firmly.

"I'm not Gia," she spat. "Gia was a scared little girl who died in a fire. I will *never* be Gia again."

"Look, we need to get you out of here before the hospital starts trying to find out your identity for your insurance," Fletcher said.

"Wait," Logan said quickly. "You can't just take her out of here. She's still being watched by the doctors. She still needs care."

"She's stable enough for transport, right?" Gunner said. "We have a doctor who will help her."

"I know it's not my place," Logan argued, "but that seems like a terrible idea. I'll pay for whatever care she needs. She doesn't have to use insurance at all."

"You're not really in any position to be making decisions for our sister," Fletcher said. "You're the reason she's here in the first place."

Logan's mouth dropped open slightly. "Your sister?" He looked to Fiona. "I didn't realize these were your brothers."

She nodded.

"How did this man find you, anyway? Why would you keep my sister in the same town where you had a madman chasing you?"

"It wasn't the same town," he said. "We're miles away. I'm from Woodward, Oklahoma. I met your sister in Tennessee."

"Where were you headed?" Gunner asked.

"I don't know," Logan said honestly. "Truth be told, I don't think she even knew. We were just trying to get somewhere safe. Obviously, I was running...but she never told me what she was running from. She didn't tell me much at all."

"That still doesn't answer the question of how the guy found you."

Logan shook his head. "It was stupid. I don't know how

he found me, but I do know that yesterday morning I chose to use my credit card for the first time since I'd disappeared. From the research I'd found on the guy, he was an IT expert. He owned his own company. I'd been very careful about using my money just in case he'd managed to be keeping tabs on it."

"You used your card for last night?" Fiona asked, wrinkling her forehead at him.

"What was last night?" Fletcher asked.

"Why would you do that?" Fiona stared at him, her brow lowered.

"Because you're worth it," he answered. "But, also because I got careless. I wasn't afraid anymore. That's what you do for me. You make it so I'm not afraid of anything. Except losing you."

"Well, smooth move, buttercup. You almost got her killed," Fletcher said.

"That's not fair, Fletch," Fiona said defensively.

"It doesn't matter. We have to get both of you out of here now," Gunner said, pointing to Fiona and Fletcher. "Can you check the door? Make sure there's no one coming."

"I don't understand. What's going on?" Logan asked.

"Do you want to tell him?" Fletcher asked, raising a brow at Fiona. "Can we trust him?"

Fiona shook her head. Did she want to tell him? No. Could she trust him? She still wasn't sure. "Can I have a minute with him?" she asked.

Fletcher looked unsure, but Gunner nodded. "Quickly. We're going to get the car and move it to the front. You have, like, five minutes, Fiona."

She nodded, watching as her brothers left the room.

Logan walked closer to her. "I don't like the idea of you leaving. You need to stay here until your doctor clears you."

"How long will that be?" she asked.

"I don't know. Hours, maybe? A day?"

"I don't have a day. I might not even have hours. I know you think you've got me all figured out, Logan, but the truth is you've barely scratched the surface." She took a deep breath. "I am not who you think I am. Literally and figuratively. I'm not someone you can save. In fact, I've spent all my life trying to save others...and it has done nothing but destroy me. So, I have to go with my brothers now. Because, if anyone understands my level of fucked up, it's them. And you have to leave. Because I can't drag you down with me. Because I can't hurt you like I've hurt them." She reached for his hand, squeezing it once. "But mostly because I can't afford to have anyone else in my life that I could grow to care about. I'm not worthy of love, Logan. I'm not even capable of love. I'm this...this tomb of secrets. I'm bursting at the seams with secrets and lies and coverups, and I can't have someone around who I have to censor myself around."

"You don't have to censor yourself around me."

"I do," she said. "Because I don't want to be your patient. I care about you. I care about you in a way I've never let myself care about anyone. And that terrifies me. Not because I'm some sensitive little girl who got my heart broken and I'm terrified to let it happen again. But because I've been ripped to shreds by life, destroyed and burned by love, and in turn, I ruin everything in my wake. I can't let that happen to you. I'm dangerous to those who matter to me."

He wiped a tear from her cheek with his fingertip.

"Fiona, I don't care if you destroy me. I don't care. Because losing you will destroy me even worse. Believe it or not, since Serena, you've been the only good thing in my life. You're the only thing that makes me feel like I can go on." He sat down. "Truth be told, you're the only reason I'm still alive. When we met, I was planning to kill myself. I knew he'd find me eventually, and the idea of running—especially running alone—was enough to terrify me. But, then you came along. And I saw the brokeness in you. I thought you needed me, and that gave me purpose. Purpose I hadn't felt since I had to quit my job. I loved being a doctor, Fiona. Because it gave me a reason to live. *You* gave me a reason to live when I had nothing else. And I meant it when I said I was falling for you. Because I'm just as messed up as you are. In the most beautiful way possible, we are good together. At our worst moments, we can help heal each other. Like you've already done for me. Like I hope to be able to do for you."

She froze, listening to his words and thinking back to their time together. It was true. Since she'd known Logan, she'd been feeling more normal than she had for most of her life. It was the closest thing to a normal relationship she'd ever had.

"What do you live for, Fiona? You've fought so hard to live. To survive. I can see that. So, what is it you're living for if not to find love? Or at least happiness? Isn't that what we're all looking for? Isn't that what makes this all worth it? All the heartache and darkness...for just the hope that somewhere out there...something better is waiting? I want to be your better. Because I think you might be mine." He took her hand, placing it on his cheek.

She shook her head. "I don't know."

"You don't—"

"I don't know what I'm living for anymore. Used to be for Fletcher. To keep him safe. Alive. But, now he's moved on...he's happy. And I'm just alone."

"You aren't alone. Not if you don't want to be."

"It's not the same."

"It doesn't have to be the same. But, it can be beautiful nonetheless."

She adjusted in the bed, pulling her hand from his face. "For so long, practically my whole life, I've focused on saving my brother. And now, he's safe. So, what do I do? I just pretend I haven't done all the horrible things I've done to save him? Just forget they happened? Just pretend I don't have nightmares? Forget that I'm so empty it scares me?"

He stared at her, his eyes searching her face before he spoke. "Fiona, you can't save anyone else until you've been brave enough to save yourself."

"I don't know how to do that," she said, her voice soft. She looked away, wrapping her arms around herself.

"You can start by telling me the truth. Just speaking your secrets out loud takes their power away."

"How do you know that?"

"It's what I do," he said with a smirk. "Let me save you."

"My name didn't used to be Fiona," she said, feeling the lump leaving her throat as she spoke the secret that had burned inside of her for so long. "It was Gia. Before." He nodded, though he didn't speak. "But, I *am* Fiona now. I didn't lie to you about that. Those boys are my brothers. Gunner and Fletcher. Fletcher used to be Gavin. We had to run when we were little."

"And you've been running ever since?" he asked, seeming to understand.

"Our childhood was awful. My mother was horribly abusive, and my father was an alcoholic."

"Was he the one that..."

"Raped me?" she asked, numb to the word. "No. Of course not. My father was never cruel. He...I think he loved us. In his own way. He just, all he ever did was drink. We never got to know him that well."

"Where are they now?" he asked.

"Dead. My mother died a few months ago. My dad died when we were younger. Seventeen." She grimaced, not ready to tell him that story yet.

"I'm so, so—" His words were interrupted as the door swung open and Fletcher stood in front of them once again.

"We have to go. Now." He helped her stand up, Logan on the other side of her instantly. "Gunner's got the car ready."

"I want to take my car," she said firmly as she pulled the dress up over her legs to replace the hospital gown, trying to keep her body hidden.

"We can all fit in Gunner's. It's better if we go together."

"My car is the only thing I've ever bought for myself. The things I had to do to get it..." She winced. "I'm not leaving it."

"I'll drive with her," Logan said. "We'll keep right behind you."

She looked at him, wanting to argue that she wasn't going to let him drive her car, but she stopped. She wanted to trust someone. More than that, she wanted to trust Logan.

“Okay,” Fletcher said hesitantly. “If you’re sure that’s okay with you.”

“It’s okay,” Fiona agreed. “I trust him.” And for once, she sort of meant it.

TWENTY-ONE

FIONA

Fiona let Logan drive, claiming that she was too tired. In all reality, her leg was beginning to burn and sleep would've been amazing, but she couldn't convince her mind to slow down enough for her to succumb to a nap. She didn't trust him enough. Not just yet.

They followed Gunner's car closely, headed down the busy interstate. She wasn't sure exactly where they were headed, but they'd left Missouri and had passed through Tennessee already. They'd been in Georgia for a while before she realized they were heading toward Atlanta. Were they going to take her back to the clinic? Panic began to set in. She couldn't go back. She wouldn't.

Logan looked over at her. "What's wrong?" he asked, noticing her expression.

"Where are we going?"

"I don't know, why?"

"This is the way back to the clinic. I can't go back there." Her voice had grown tight as she began figuring out her exit strategy. Of course her brothers hadn't come back to help her. They were coming back to lock her up again. She'd foolishly believed they could forgive her enough to care. To want to help her. But she was wrong. They didn't care that Neville had taken advantage of her. They didn't care that she had tried to kill herself. Hell, maybe that was what they wanted anyway. Maybe it would make it easier on all of them.

"Relax," Logan whispered. "I'm not going to let them put you back there. They're your brothers. We're all going to take care of you. I promise."

"They hate me," she said with a sob. "They hate me, and they want me out of their lives."

"Fiona, they don't hate you. Do you know how worried they were about you when I called Fletcher? They were so relieved to know you were safe. *They don't hate you.*"

"You couldn't possibly know how they feel about me."

"Look, I know that you're scared, okay? Do you want me to turn off here and try to lose them? Because I will. But I don't think they want to hurt you."

"Then where are they taking me? Why are we back in Georgia?"

"You know as much as I do," he swore. "They said something about knowing a doctor. Do you have any doctors in your family? People they might trust with your secret?"

"No way. I don't know any doctors. And certainly not in Atlanta."

He reached over, taking her hand. "I promise you I'm not

going to let anything happen to you. I'll protect you at all costs. But you do need to trust me, too."

She shook her head. "Trust you? Fine, but you have to be honest with me. You never told me who it was that called you. Why you were looking for me."

He nodded. "I know. I'm going to tell you. I'm going to tell you everything—" He stopped talking, his eyes narrowing. "We're pulling off at this exit. Do you know anyone who lives near here?"

She looked at the exit sign. "No one."

They pulled off onto the exit, turning right at the stop sign behind Gunner's silver SUV. "Where in the world are we going?" she mumbled to herself.

"They seem to have a plan," he whispered, scooting closer to the windshield as if he were trying to see their destination from there.

After a few silent moments filled with worry, the SUV turned down a small gravel road. The road was long and uninhabited, surrounded by trees and deer and absolutely nothing else. When they came to the end of the drive, Fiona laid eyes on a large, cabin-style home. It had a big wraparound porch with a wooden swing. As their cars pulled into the drive, the front door swung open and a round, auburn-haired woman stood on the porch. Behind her, a blond man walked out, placing a hand around her waist. When they climbed from their cars, a black girl with shoulder-length hair came hurrying from the house and into Fletcher's arms. It was the girl Fiona had saved. She'd survived somehow. Fiona felt a small smile grow on her lips. Seconds later, Reagan appeared, hurrying to hug Gunner, and her smile disappeared. She wouldn't be welcome here. Not like this. What were her brothers thinking?

Fletcher turned, taking Fiona's hand and leading her up the walk and onto the porch. As they walked, he introduced her to everyone.

"This is Vaida, my fiancée," he said. "Vaida, this is my sister, Fiona."

"I hear I owe you my life," she said, leaning in to hug Fiona. Fiona was stiff in her arms, not moving to hug her back. She was waiting for them to admit this had all been a trick. Waiting for them to tell her they were better off without her.

"You know Reagan, of course," Fletcher said, his voice cautious. "This is—"

"Jesse Mathis," Fiona said, recognizing him as they grew closer.

"Yeah, it's good to see you," he said, though he kept one protective shoulder in front of the auburn-haired woman.

"You're...Quinn, right?" she asked. "I'm sorry, I don't remember your last name."

"Quinn...well, it used to be Reynolds. It's Mathis, now," she said, patting Jesse's chest and stepping out from behind him with her protruding belly.

"What are we doing here?" she asked Fletcher. Gunner kept close to Reagan, his body separating her from Fiona.

"Jesse's going to take care of you until you're better."

"What? Why?"

"He's a surgeon," Quinn answered. "And I'm a nurse. We're going to take good care of you." She smiled politely, but Fiona knew something was off.

"But, why? Why here? Why are you all here?"

"Because we're going to take care of you, Fiona," Fletcher said. "Because I should've been taking better care of you all along. When we heard you broke out...we came here. Jesse's place was secluded, and we could keep everyone safe here."

"Safe?"

"From you," Reagan answered, her voice carrying across the porch.

"What are you talking about? Did you think I broke out to hurt you?"

"We didn't know what to think, Fiona," Gunner said harshly. "The last time we saw you wasn't exactly a happy homecoming."

Fiona locked her jaw, crossing her arms. "Which is exactly why I shouldn't be here. I didn't ask for your help. Any of you." She turned around, walking to Logan's side. "I don't want to hurt anyone. That was never my plan. But, it's obvious I don't belong here, so I'll—" She gasped, bending down and holding her leg. "Ouch, *shit.*"

Jesse was at her side in an instant. "Are you okay? What hurts?"

"I'm...ouch...I'm fine. It's just sore." She grasped her leg, trying to lift it.

"It's really warm," Jesse said. "We need to get you inside. It could be infected."

"It's fine, honestly."

"Fiona," Fletcher said firmly. "Get in the house. You aren't leaving until you're healthy. It's not up for discussion." He pointed toward the door, though his eyes softened as hers did. She allowed Logan and Jesse to put their shoulders under her arms, practically carrying her into the house. "And you two, I know it's hard, but if you're going to be here, you have to be civil." He looked between his brother and Reagan. "Please."

Gunner nodded, looking to Reagan before speaking. "Fine."

Quinn shut the door as they all entered. "I've got the guest room all set up if you want to put her in there."

"No," Gunner said firmly. "I want her where we can see her."

"Gunner—" Fletcher started to argue.

"The couch is fine," Fiona said, letting out a sigh as they set her onto it. She winced as Jesse lifted her leg up, resting it on the ottoman.

"Quinn, do you have some clothes we can put on her? Get her out of this dress?" Jesse asked over his shoulder.

Quinn nodded, waddling away. "I'm sure I can find something."

"The rest of you, settle in," he said. "We're gonna be here for a while."

TWENTY-TWO

FIONA

Fiona lay on the couch, Logan at her feet on the floor. The rest of the house had fallen silent, each of the couples retiring to their bedrooms. Logan kept a close eye on her, jumping at her every move, offering her food, drinks, or medicine every chance he got.

He rubbed her ankle, watching her. "I'm sorry about all of this," he said softly.

"All of what?" she asked.

"I should've never approached you at that gas station."

"Don't say that."

"If I hadn't, you wouldn't have gotten shot. You wouldn't be put in this situation, which is painful to say the least. I know how uncomfortable you must be."

"Look, Logan, I'm never going to be one of those mushy people. I'm never going to say sweet things to you or expect you to say them to me. I'm just not that way. That's not something you can fix."

"I'm not—"

"*That being said*, I'm incredibly glad you approached me at that gas station. I wouldn't change it."

He smiled. "Really?"

"Don't get weird on me," she said with a laugh.

"I just don't understand why, out of everyone, Gunner seems to be the most mad at you. Fletcher's the one who you...you know..." He trailed off. "Right?"

"Yeah, I killed Fletcher's girlfriend," she said, her eyes going dark. "She was Gunner's wife's sister."

"Oh."

"And Gunner does what Reagan does." She paused, taking a breath. "I also tried to kill *her*. Reagan. And their daughter."

"Oh," he repeated, looking away from her for the first time. "Geez, this family is complicated."

"You have no idea."

"Why would you do that?" he asked, keeping his voice unaccusing. He was incredibly good at making horrible conversations seem ordinary.

"I don't know why," she said, her voice cracking. "I mean, I do know why, but it isn't logical. I was scared. They had found out the truth about me, and I was terrified the news would make it back to my mother. I was scared she'd come after me. She was...she was evil, Logan. I don't know how else to describe it. Her every waking moment was spent making sure my life was miserable. And miserable is putting it lightly."

"I'm sorry, Fiona."

"It's no excuse," she said. "I know it's not. It's just...it's the only reason I have." She began crying then, silent tears trailing down her face. "I think I might be crazy."

Logan climbed onto the couch next to her, rubbing her face with his palms. "Hey, do you want to know a secret?"

She nodded.

"Crazy people don't wonder if they're crazy," he whispered, kissing her forehead.

She looked up, feeling his lips on her skin and then on her mouth, and allowing him to kiss her again. She wrapped a hand around his neck, her tears hitting his cheeks. "It's okay, Fiona. I promise you it's all going to be okay."

"How can you promise that? How can you promise anything? The people I love, the people I would die for, they all hate me."

"We can fix that."

"It's too late."

"If there's anything I have learned in this life, it's that it's never too late. Certainly not for this. I've seen how your brothers look at you. When you start to fall, they lean your way. When you speak, they listen. They may be mad at you. You may have really hurt them. But they don't hate you, Fiona."

She covered her eyes, allowing more tears to fall. "What if I hate myself?"

He pressed his forehead to hers, their eyes meeting again. "Now, that is something I can understand. You know all the stories about how you have to love yourself before anyone can love you?"

She nodded. "Yeah."

"It's bullshit."

"What?" She giggled.

"It's complete and utter bullshit. You don't have to love yourself, Fiona. You don't. Not yet, anyway. What you need is someone to show you how to love yourself. Someone to show you what love is supposed to be."

"And that someone is you?" She raised her eyebrows.

"No," he said with a scoff. "Haven't you been listening? I suck at love. But, maybe...just maybe that makes it work somehow. Maybe the fact that we are both insanely bad at relationships and love and, well, life in general, maybe that somehow means we're perfect for each other. Who else ever could be?"

She shook her head. "I don't know if my life will ever be calm enough for me to even consider something as frivolous as love."

"Is love frivolous?"

"When you've spent your whole life merely trying to make it from one day to the next alive, yes. Everything but surviving is frivolous."

"What are you still running from?" he asked finally. "You said it was your mother before, but she's gone. I can understand wanting to run from your past, but no one's looking for you anymore. Right? You're safe, Fiona. So, why are you still running? Who are you hiding from?"

She placed her face in her palms, feeling fresh tears in her eyes. "Myself."

"Yourself?" he asked. "Because you can't forgive yourself for what you've done?"

She shook her head. "Because I can't even...I can't catch my breath when I think about what I've done. It's...horrible. It makes me sick. *I* make myself sick."

"Fiona, you've done horrible things. I won't argue with you about that. But people make mistakes when they're scared. Yeah, your mistakes are worse than the average person, but you are still a person. You still deserve forgiveness if you're truly remorseful. Now, I said earlier you don't have to love yourself for anyone to love you back, but you do need to forgive yourself first in order to get forgiveness from anyone else."

"I can't forgive myself." Her answer was instant. It was the one thing she was sure of.

"Fletcher and Gunner will come around. They'll forgive you. But, you do have to forgive yourself. All you can do is move forward and try to be better than you were before. The first step is accepting what you've done."

"Fletcher and Gunner aren't the only ones I need forgiveness from."

"Reagan, then? We can work on all of them. We can show them that you want to change."

"Not Reagan, either," she whispered. "I mean, yes. I want forgiveness from everyone I've hurt, and the list is long. Of course I do. But, there's still someone I can never get forgiveness from."

"Who's that?"

Her eyes went dark as the memories flooded her. "The first person I ever hurt."

TWENTY-THREE

GIA
SEVENTEEN YEARS OLD

Gia stared at the stick in her hands, clad with two bright pink lines. She felt sick to her stomach, though she was unsure if that was from the life growing inside of her or the shock of it all. Maybe a little of both.

She stood up from the toilet, pulling up her pants and standing over the sink. She glared at herself in the mirror with absolutely no idea what she was going to do. How on earth was she going to make it through this? Who could she ever tell? How would she ever tell them?

She flushed the toilet, shoving the test into its box, and that box into a bag. She hid the bag underneath her t-shirt and walked out of the room. Her mother stood in the kitchen, pouring her father's drink.

"What are you looking at?" she asked hatefully.

Gia looked away. "Sorry, nothing." She shoved open her

bedroom door, walking into it and tossing the bag under the bed before the door opened again.

"You're acting weird," Misty said, looking around the room. "What are you up to?"

"Nothing," she said quickly, looking behind her.

"Mhm, fat chance." Misty stared over her shoulder, searching for the answer. She crossed her arms, frowning.

"Is that all?" Gia asked, staring at the door. She wanted nothing more than for her mother to leave the room. She couldn't catch her breath, couldn't think straight.

"Excuse me?"

Gia realized her mistake as soon as she'd asked it. "I'm sorry. I didn't mean it like that. I just...I need to study."

"Why? 'Cause you think that brain of yours is gonna get you into college?" She cackled loudly, as if it were the funniest thing in the world.

"No."

"That's right, no. You wouldn't make it so far as the door in college, Gia. Your brothers aren't going. You sure can't."

Gia nodded. "I didn't mean that. I just...I don't want to fail this test."

"You won't make it out of this town, kid. You'll be stuck here just like me for the rest of your life, and you'll look back and think...why the hell did I waste my time caring if I passed or failed?"

Gia nodded again, not meeting her mother's eye.

"Isn't that right?"

"Yeah, you're right."

"Good," Misty said, "because I think it's about time we cleaned out the refrigerator."

"What? I just did it last week!" Gia whined.

"Well, then I guess it won't be too dirty, will it?" She grabbed hold of the back of her daughter's neck, her nails digging into her skin. "All you'll ever be good for is a housewife, Gia. It's my job to teach you how to do that. Don't you want me to help you learn?"

"Yes," Gia said softly, whimpering as her mother's grasp grew tighter.

"I can't hear you."

"Yes, I want you to teach me," she said louder.

Her mother pressed her nose into her daughter's. "I don't care how much money your grandmother leaves you, you'll never see a dime of it. That money is mine, Gia. Do you hear me? If you think you're gonna run off and go to college and leave your mother in the dust, you couldn't be more wrong."

"I don't plan to do that," she promised. "I don't."

Her mother let her neck go, her eyes suddenly locked on something behind her. Her throat grew dry as Misty dashed across the room. She bent down. "What is this?" Gia watched in horror as her mother pulled the gray plastic sack from underneath the bed, fishing out the pink box. She read the words across the box aloud, before looking at her daughter in horror. "You're pregnant?"

Gia bit her lip, nodding slightly.

Misty dropped the box, launching at her daughter with her hand raised. She swung, the back of her hand connecting loudly with Gia's cheek. Gia took a step back, covering her face defensively. "What is wrong with you?" her mother spat. "What could you have possibly been thinking? This is exactly why I never let you leave this house. This. This is why I tried to keep you home. To protect you from exactly this. What will people think?" She covered her mouth, staring at her daughter. "Who's the father?" she asked finally. "Does he have money? Will he take care of you?"

Gia shook her head, not wanting to admit the truth. Could she even be sure who the father was? How could she explain that to her mother? To anyone? The whole night was a complete blur. She couldn't remember who had been where and, to be honest, she didn't want to. The whole memory was painful, it burned her stomach just to think about.

"He's not going to be involved," she whispered.

"You're wrong about that," her mother bellowed. She reached for Gia again, squeezing her cheeks and shoving her into the wall, her skull hitting with a thud. She cried out. "If you think you're going to let any man get you pregnant and then walk away you're dead wrong. Nope. Not happening. You'll tell me who he is right this instant. Or I'll ask your brothers. I'm sure you've bragged about all your little whore-adventures to them."

She could taste her blood in her mouth, her cheeks rubbing roughly against her teeth as her mother's grip continue to stay firm. "Mom, please," she cried, trying to remove her hands, though she couldn't. She knew better. When her mother was mad, she wielded a vice-like grip.

"Who is he?" she demanded, her lips inches from her daughter's.

"I...I don't know."

She let go of her face, allowing Gia to drop to the floor. She clutched her cheeks, wincing from the pain that remained. Misty stared down at her.

"What do you mean you don't know?"

Gia shook her head, unable to speak the words. "I'll have

an abortion," she swore. "I'll get it taken care of. I swear I will."

"And who will pay for that?" she demanded.

"I'll work it out," she promised. "You won't have to worry about it."

Misty moved toward her and Gia cowered, crying before her mother had even swung. But, eventually she did, her hand connecting with her cheek once again. This time, Gia's face slammed into the wall, and she was sure it would bruise.

"I'm not stupid, Gia. And I'm not leaving this up to you. You will give me a name right now." She wagged her finger in her daughter's face.

"I don't know," she screamed back to her mother, her face growing warm with fury. Misty reeled back, surprised by her sudden outburst. "I was raped," she admitted, letting a sob escape her chest. "Okay? I was raped by several boys from school. So, I don't know who the father is. And, even if I did, there's no way in hell he'd be coming near me or this baby ever."

Misty stared at her, and Gia hoped she might see some shred of humanity in her dark eyes. Finally, Misty let out a loud laugh, clutching her stomach for emphasis.

"What's so funny?" Gia demanded.

Misty stormed past her, still laughing dramatically. "Nice try, Gia. Who would ever want to rape you?"

TWENTY-FOUR

GIA
SEVENTEEN YEARS OLD

The next day, Gia woke with a swollen cheek and a sore jaw. Neither of her brothers had come home the night before, and she'd stayed up most of the night listening for any sound that might mean her mother was coming back for her. Luckily, Misty had gone to bed early and had stayed there most of the night.

Gia climbed out of bed, hearing Gunner's car roaring into the driveway. She listened carefully as he stormed into the house, talking angrily with Misty, and then she heard his door shut.

She stood from her bed, walking carefully to his room. She needed to tell Gunner the truth. To get him to find the way out. She swung open his bedroom door and took a deep breath, preparing to deliver the news. She stopped, realizing he was packing a bag. "Gunner?" she asked, tears filling her eyes.

"Where are you going?" He couldn't leave her. She wouldn't survive it.

He shoved what remained in one drawer into the bag before looking up. "What happened to you?" he asked.

"I'm fine," she dismissed him, her hand moving to her cheek for a second. "Where were you last night? Gavin never came home, either." He didn't stop moving, filling his bag with anything he could grab. When she realized he wasn't going to answer, she went on. "You're leaving, aren't you?"

He nodded, looking at her finally. "It's time."

"Take me with you," she begged, more tears suddenly in her eyes.

He stopped then, approaching her and brushing a thumb over her bruised cheek. "I'm sorry, Gia, I can't."

"You can't leave us," she cried, panic filling her voice.

"I can't stay here anymore. I'm sorry. I know I promised you...but I can't. And I can't take you with me. You have school. I can't take care of you." He shook his head, stepping back and stuffing a few remaining things into the duffel bag.

Panic began to set in at the idea of him leaving. Gavin and Gunner were all she had. Well, besides this baby. She touched her stomach. This baby would need an uncle. She would need someone to help her. He had to stay. "It'll get worse," she pleaded with him. "It'll all get worse without you here, Gun. You protect us. We're safe as long as you're here."

He slammed a drawer shut. "Safe? Gia, look at you. I'm not protecting you from anything. The only way I know to protect you is to go to the police. Do you want to do that? 'Cause I'll take you right now."

She lowered her head. "You know I can't." If she went to the police, there was a good chance they wouldn't believe her.

And then what? Things would get worse. Much worse. And, if they didn't, Misty might convince the police it was Rick hurting them. Her father may not have been perfect, but he'd never physically hurt them. She couldn't let him go down for her mother's crimes. And Misty had made it clear long ago that she'd make sure that's exactly what would happen. Gia had seen it firsthand, how convincing her mother could be. How easy it was for her to manipulate those around her.

"Then what am I supposed to do? I'm not going to keep sitting around waiting for him to kill one of you," Gunner said, staring at her.

"Maybe that wouldn't be the worst thing." She hadn't meant to let the words slip out of her mouth. The words that were always there in the back of her mind. How easy it would be to end it. To make it all stop. How easy it would be to say goodbye to all the pain and darkness, to never have another bruise, to never let her mother destroy her mental peace again. To have nothing. To be nothing. To feel nothing.

"What are you talking about?"

"I'd rather die than keep living this way." Her voice was firm, her eyes swimming with tears. It was the closest she'd ever come to admitting the truth. She could tell Gunner about the pills she'd stashed in the back of her dresser. The ones she kept just in case the day came when she'd had enough.

"You don't mean that." She saw the judgement in his eyes. He thought she was being dramatic.

"I'm a prisoner, Gunner. Of course I do."

"You only have another year and you'll be free. Just one more year."

"Don't you see how screwed up we are? We will never be free."

"Gia, please don't talk like that. After you graduate, I'll be settled somewhere. Then you can come with me. I'll keep you safe."

"And Gavin?" she asked, her eyes filled with hope. She couldn't go without Gavin.

"Gavin can take care of himself," he said through gritted teeth.

No. She couldn't go without him. Gunner and Gavin's relationship had always been strange—riddled with jealousy and misunderstanding, but at the end of the day, they'd always been brothers. That was what was most important. "He's in as much danger as I am."

"Gavin would protect himself if it came down to it. He'd choose himself over you. Don't let him fool you."

"He's our brother," she said under her breath, feeling his words slap her. Gavin would never choose to hurt her. He loved her.

"He's a self-righteous, selfish prick, Gia. Open your eyes," he yelled, his face growing red.

"Don't you yell at me," she snapped. "If you weren't so quick to judge him, maybe the two of you could get along. He's not so bad, Gun." If they could get along, the three of them could protect each other. If Gunner would take their side over their mother's even once, if he would see through her façade, Gavin would trust him enough to allow Gia to tell Gunner the truth. That might be enough to save them. But, she couldn't do it unless Gavin believed he'd side with them. That was likely never going to happen.

He huffed. "Fat chance."

"You guys let your big heads get in the way. You're brothers. And you need each other. But neither of you can see that."

"We don't," he said sharply. "We've never needed each other. And we never will. I don't have time to have this argument with you again."

"Please don't do this, Gunner. I need you." She pressed her hands together, as if in prayer, begging him to stay.

He rubbed his chin, looking directly at her after a moment. His expression was stern. "Fine. Pack a bag. Necessities only. We leave in fifteen minutes."

She shook her head, realizing she wasn't going to convince him to stay. "I can't."

"What? You just said that's what you wanted."

"Not without him."

"You're choosing him?" he asked, his eyes full of sorrow.

She nodded firmly. "I will always choose him. He's my brother."

"I thought I was, too," he said, his voice soft as he stormed away from her. He was slipping away. She realized she may never see him again if she couldn't convince him to stay now.

"Gunner, wait!" she yelled, chasing him through the house. "Please!"

Misty appeared in front of them, a frown on her wrinkled face. "What do you two think you're doing? What's with all the yelling? You're going to wake your daddy."

"I'm leaving, Momma," Gunner told her, his voice low.

"Leaving? What do you mean?"

"I'm out. Done. This is goodbye."

"Quit being dramatic. What's going on?" his mother asked, confusion on her face.

He took hold of her frail, bony shoulders and hugged her tight. "I'm leaving Dale," he said, "and I won't ever be back."

"You can't leave us," she said, her eyes wild with fear.

Behind them, Gia's sobs could be heard. "Please, Gunner," she begged.

"He'll kill us all," his mother warned. "If you leave, we're as good as dead." Gia rolled her eyes, though it went unnoticed by everyone. The mere idea of being in a house without Gunner, her only defense against Misty's insanity, was terrifying.

"Then, come with me. We'll leave right now. By the time he notices, we'll be long gone."

"No," Misty silenced him, her voice quiet. "It won't work, Gun. Not like this."

"I won't stay another night in this town. Come with me or not, either way I'm leaving right now."

He waited for them to respond, and when neither did, he hugged them both at once, his jaw strangely tight. "I'll do whatever I can to take care of you, I promise," he said, though Gia knew he couldn't make such promises. "But I have to go."

"I love you," Gia said, kissing his cheek and accepting her fate. "I understand," she whispered in his ear, "and I forgive you. This isn't your fault."

When she pulled away, his eyes were empty. He might as well have already been gone. Gia broke eye contact, feeling sick to her stomach. He took her face in his hands, kissing her head. "I'm going to take care of you. I promise I'll be back for you."

She nodded, watching as he walked out of the door. As it shut, she turned to walk away, trying hard not to cry. A fist made contact with the back of her head, hurling her to the floor. She fell onto the carpet with a thud, letting out a loud yelp.

"What did you do?" Misty screeched.

"I didn't do anything," Gia called back, rubbing her lip. She tasted blood, but she couldn't be sure where it was coming from. She rolled over, scooting backward and trying hard to stand.

"Get up," Misty called, waving her hand as if Gia was just too much work to abuse. She turned and walked into the kitchen, grabbing a clear tumbler and filling it with whiskey. She took a drink herself before topping it off and opening the bottle of pills. She smiled at Gia, a menacing smile that warned of what was to come. She laid four pills out, crushing them carefully and sprinkling them into his drink. "Now, be a dear and go give this to your daddy. I've got to run to the store and get more. I won't be gone long. You aren't to leave."

Gia nodded, holding the glass with both shaking hands. "Okay." With that, her mother shoved past her, grabbing the car keys from the counter and slamming the front door behind her. Gia watched in horror as her mother pulled out of the driveway, only feeling relief as she disappeared down the road. She stared at the drink in her hand, half-tempted to drink it herself. If whatever the pills did was enough to knock her father out each night, she couldn't imagine what it might do to her.

Thinking of that made her think of the pills in her drawer. How easy it would be to take them. She stared into the drink, watching the white powder swirl around the bottom. Finally, she walked to the sink, pouring the drink down the drain and carrying the empty glass into her father's bedroom.

"Dad?" she called, knocking on the door before entering.

He wiped his chin with his arm, sitting up at seeing her worried expression. "What is it, sweetheart? What's the matter?"

She walked to the bed. "Momma wanted me to bring you a drink," she said, holding out the tumbler. "But I couldn't."

"What do you mean?"

"I need to tell you the truth, Dad. And I need you to care."

"What truth, Gia?" He stared at her, his head hung to the side.

"About Momma. And about you. About everything."

He patted the bed. "Sit down, sweetheart. You're scaring me." When she sat down, Rick stared at her cheek. "I'm so sorry, baby." He reached up to touch it. "I swear I'm going to get help."

She pushed his hand away. "Dad, stop. That's what I want to talk to you about. You didn't do this."

"What do you mean?"

"It wasn't you. It's never been you."

"Of course it has. Your mother has told me how I get when I drink. I know the monster I become..." He paused. "But I never meant to become this way. I never wanted to hurt you."

"Dad, listen to me. You aren't the one hurting us. Honestly, you're not."

"I don't understand."

"It's Momma. It's Momma who hurts us."

"No," he said softly, his voice growing higher. "No."

"Yes. She puts pills in the drinks she gives me to give to you. And then she hurts us. She convinces you that you're the one doing it, but it's not you."

"Gia, your mother would never do that. She's harmless."

"Harmless? You've seen the way she manipulates us all. How easily she controls our lives. It's...I think it's what makes her happy."

Rick sat, seeming to take it all in. "But, why?"

She shook her head. "I don't know. And, more importantly, we don't have time to figure it out. She won't be gone long, and I need your help."

He rubbed his tired eyes. "Okay."

"Dad, I'm pregnant."

"You're...you're what?"

"I'm pregnant," she said matter-of-factly. "And Momma is going to end up hurting me enough to lose this baby." She put a hand over her stomach. "I have to get out of here."

He shook his head. "Out of here? What do you mean?"

"Gunner's gone," she whispered. "He left. I want to go, too."

"Where's he gone?"

"I don't know," she said honestly.

"And you want to go with him?"

"No," she said. "I can't go without Gavin, and they would never go with each other."

"So, what are you asking me for?"

"I want you to help me run away. Me and Gavin. I want to leave."

"Sweetheart, I just...I can't see how that would be possible. You're only seventeen. You're not old enough to take care of yourself out there."

"I have to," she whispered. "I have to protect myself. And this baby. What choice do I have?"

He stared at her cheek. "Your mother really did this?"

She nodded.

"It wasn't me?"

"No."

He frowned, obviously thinking. "Even not knowing that she was hurting you, I do know that your mother would never let you leave. She would track you down. She's persistent, Gia. She doesn't give in, and she doesn't back down."

She bowed her head. "I know."

He patted her on the shoulder. "It's going to be okay. I'm going to help you, sweetheart. I am. I just...we have to be smart about this."

She looked up at him; it was unusual to have her father be so coherent. So tender. So...fatherly.

"I'm so sorry, Gia. I wish I had known. I wish I could've stopped it years ago." His voice cracked as he stared at her. "I'm just so sorry."

She nodded, though she didn't respond. What was there to possibly say? It's okay? It wasn't. Nothing was okay. Nothing would be okay unless she got out. And this was her only chance to make that happen.

"Please just...please just help me save us."

He nodded, his eyes widening. "I have an idea," he said hesitantly. "But it's insane."

"I'll do anything."

"I'm going to get out with you, Gia. I'll take you and your brother...we're going to get somewhere safe until we can figure everything out."

She bit her lip, surprised by the relief she felt. "Okay. How?"

"When I was little, I used to love to blow stuff up in my backyard," he said quietly. "Did I ever tell you that?"

"No," she said, shaking her head. "Why are *you telling me that?" She was almost afraid to ask.*

"Because, Gia. Because in order to leave, we're going to have to die."

TWENTY-FIVE

GIA
SEVENTEEN YEARS OLD

When Gavin got home, he was distraught. She pulled him into the bedroom quickly, before Misty could see him.

"What's wrong, Gav?" she demanded. Gunner had left that morning, and after her talk with her father, Reagan had shown up, obviously upset. Now Gavin was also in a panic. What in the world was happening?

He put his head down. "I ruined everything."

"What are you talking about? What did you ruin?"

"Everything, Gia." He placed his clenched fists over his eyes. "Everything."

"Quit being dramatic," she snapped. She had planned to tell him about the baby, about the plan for that night, but Rick had made her swear to keep it all a secret. Gavin had never been good with secrets. He was too soft. Too trusting. The world hadn't broken him yet. He was still in his cloud of

popularity and good looks, even Misty abuse didn't seem to be enough to bring him down. "What happened?"

"I can't tell you. It makes me sick, Gia." He sank onto his bed. "I just...I can't talk about it."

She hugged him carefully. "You can tell me anything, Gav. You know that."

He nodded, wiping a tear from his eyes. "I almost slept with Reagan."

"You what?"

"It wasn't on purpose. I didn't mean to. I was drunk, and it just sort of happened."

"Is that why she had your truck?" she asked.

"Yes. She took it. I let her. Gunner's never going to forgive me, Gia. Never. He'll never trust me again, and how can I blame him?"

"Gavin, calm down," she said, rubbing his shoulder. "We're going to figure this all out. It's hardly all your fault. You were drunk. What was Reagan's excuse?"

He put his face in his palm, groaning. "She was asleep. It was dark. I'm a moron. I haven't even gotten to talk to Holly. What will she think? She's going to break up with me. I can't lose her, Gia. I think I love her." He stared at her with fear in his eyes, and she knew she had to break his heart.

"None of that matters anymore, Gav. We aren't going to be seeing any of them ever again."

"What do you mean?" he demanded, his voice too loud.

"Shh," she shushed him. "Keep your voice down."

"What are you talking about, Gia? What are you planning?"

"We're getting out of here."

"Who?"

She thought about her father, about the fear in his eyes when he'd told her not to tell. Gavin couldn't be trusted, he'd said. Not that he'd mean to slip up, but he would. Secrets just weren't his thing. "Me and you," she whispered. "I can't tell you anything else. You're just going to have to trust me, okay?"

"Gia, I can't leave Holly."

"You slept with her sister. She's not going to forgive you. You have to know that."

His jaw went tight. "I can try. I'm not going to give up on us like that."

She took his face in her hands, staring into his eyes and forcing him to see hers. "Gavin, I'm asking you as your sister, your best friend, and the only one who's been there for you through everything...I need you to do this for me. It's going to hurt. It's going to break your heart. I know that. I know what I'm asking of you. But, I have to get out. I'm not going to survive here." She pressed her lips together, stressing her next words carefully. "I will die if I have to stay here any longer."

He closed his eyes, another tear falling. When he looked back up, his expression was stony. "Okay."

"Okay?"

"Just tell me what to do, and I'll do it."

She nodded. "I've got a plan. You're just going to have to trust me."

"I do trust you, Gia. I always will."

TWENTY-SIX

GIA
SEVENTEEN YEARS OLD

Gia walked into her father's room with the tumbler of whiskey her mother had prepared in her hand. He was in bed waiting for her. She handed the glass over, her hands shaking.

He took it, setting it on the end table. "Did you get everything I told you to?"

"Yes, we have it ready."

"And your brother still doesn't know the plan?"

"No," she said. "He's worked out some of it, but I haven't told him everything."

"Good, you can tell him now. Just keep him in your room; don't let him talk to your mother," he said, reaching across and squeezing her hand. "After you do it, you two run as far and as fast as you can. I'll meet you at the park. Stay in the woods. Stay hidden. Don't come out until you see me. Do you understand? No one can see you."

"Okay," she said, her voice low.

"I'm going to get us out of here. Last night was the last time you'll ever have to be afraid." He kissed her forehead carefully. "Things are going to get better for us."

She nodded. "Thank you."

He let out a sigh. "No, thank you, Gia. Thank you for finally telling me the truth. You have no idea the weight your mother's lie had on me. The idea that I was hurting my children..." He paused. "And you are my children. Even if our blood says otherwise."

She felt tears forming in her eyes and blinked them away rapidly. It was the first time they'd discussed the fact that she and her brother weren't biologically his.

"You'd better go," he whispered. "Before she comes in." He kissed her head again. "I'll see you soon. Take care of yourselves."

GIA AND GAVIN *climbed out of the window just seconds before the small explosion. They'd done it at the exact time Rick had instructed her to, the time that would allow them all to get out safely, leaving only Misty still in the house. They'd carefully laid their clothes out, Gavin's watch, and other things. Just enough to let the police think they had been there. That they had died there. Her father was going to do the same.*

They raced through the empty field, hurrying into the shadows of the woods. The heat from the fire was reaching them, even from where they were now. It was hot and getting hotter as the fire continued to spread.

"Where do we go?" Gavin asked.

"Over here," Gia told him. "Come on." She shoved him back further, headed for the park. They ran as fast and as hard as their legs would carry them, panicking every time a car drew near. Someone jogged past them on the road, but they were careful not to be seen, frozen in their spot. They heard the sirens headed their way, watching the fire trucks, cop cars, and ambulance as they zoomed past, headed for their house.

Would it work? Gia couldn't be sure. Would their mother survive? If she did, would she believe that they'd died? She couldn't be sure of that, either. Would she grieve her children? Now, that, Gia knew wouldn't happen. Misty wasn't capable of grief. She was, in the most basic sense, a sociopath. She couldn't be bothered to care about anyone else. Certainly not the children she'd brought into this world. Or the husband she was supposed to love.

When they reached the treeline just beyond the park, they stopped. "Rest here," Gia said, panting. She watched for her father, waiting to see his shadow walking across the field as well. They sat for minutes on end, waiting for him to hurry toward them. But he didn't. He was nowhere to be seen.

"What are we waiting for?" Gavin asked. "We need to go."

"No," she said. "We can't go yet."

"Why not?" he demanded. "We're risking being caught the longer we stay."

Gia hadn't had a chance to tell Gavin the full plan, or that their father was involved. She had planned to, but Gavin was still upset over Holly and over the whole Gunner mess. She didn't have time to explain everything, to tell him why they should trust their father when they never had before. She didn't have time to explain it to herself, either. So, as she sat watching and waiting for a man that hadn't shown up, she began replaying the night. She'd waited until just the right time, hadn't she? She hadn't rushed. Rick had made it out. He had to have.

Gavin slept against a tree after a few hours, snoring peacefully as if the nightmare hadn't happened. Gia couldn't sleep. She couldn't think straight. She paced, watching for her father. Every slight movement caught her attention. Where was he? She was sure he'd told her to meet him there. She was positive. She wouldn't have gotten that wrong.

They stayed, waiting in the woods, for another full day. Finally, Gavin had had enough. "We have to go, Gia. I don't understand what you're waiting for, but we aren't safe here. We have to leave." He grabbed her arm, attempting to pull her from the edge of the woods and deeper inside of it.

She struggled against him for a moment, knowing that if she accepted what he was saying, she was accepting something she couldn't bear to put into thoughts. Something that was burning in her brain. Something she couldn't stand to believe. But, it was true. She knew it. She knew it an hour after they'd left, maybe even sooner. And the longer they waited for Rick, the more the truth rung in her ears.

She'd messed up. She'd done something wrong. He hadn't made it out. She'd killed her own father. She'd killed the only person who had tried to save her. And she could never tell her brother that truth.

As she let him pull her into the woods, she felt something breaking in her mind. A wall forming. She couldn't feel the pain anymore. It hurt too much. She had things to figure out now. Where they were going. What they were doing. Gavin was her responsibility now. Her job was to keep him safe. And he could never know the truth about what she'd done. No one could.

A WEEK LATER, *as Gavin and Gia foraged through the woods, trying to come up with a plan, Gia felt a sharp pain in her stomach. It had been days since they'd eaten and she knew it must be from lack of food.*

After a few hours of constant pain, she realized that may not be the case. They were just outside of Dakota, a town not too far from Dale, when she announced they would need to stop for the night. They had no money and no chance of getting any, but Gia couldn't make it any further. The pain had become excruciating. They found a quiet street where they could rest for the night, lying down in a corn field. Gia felt the warmth as she lay there, trying to hide her pain from her brother. He couldn't see her hurting. If he did, she was sure he would insist they go to the hospital in order for her to get checked out. She couldn't let that happen. Instead, she lay with her back to him, biting her knuckles as the pain came in waves, radiating through her stomach and down into her thighs.

She was losing the baby. She knew that, though she wasn't sure how to feel about it. How she should feel about it. She only knew that she had to survive this. That was what mattered now. Survival. Making it to the next day and then the next. Making sure Gavin made it, too.

She could survive. Would survive. After all, look at all she'd already made it through...there was nothing this world could throw at her that she couldn't take.

TWENTY-SEVEN

GIA

SEVENTEEN YEARS OLD

The next day, Gia woke up with blood pooling between her legs. She had to figure out a way through this. She opened her bag, the only thing she'd brought with her, and pulled out clean clothes, changing quickly before Gavin woke up.

She hadn't thought to bring pads, because what on earth would she need them for during the next nine months? She rolled her eyes at her naivety. She had to come up with a plan. No more waiting for Rick to show up, no more hoping he'd survived. It was her plan now. Her idea. This had all been her. Now, she would need to see it through. They had to get out of the state. That was step one. They could continue on foot, but it would take too long. She pulled out the jewelry box her grandmother had given her. The one that she'd sworn to take good care of. Inside were cheap trinkets and odds and ends that likely weren't worth much. It was the box itself that held value. It was generations old and lined with diamonds. It was the only thing she had to remind her of her grandparents, who she'd never be able to see again.

But that didn't matter now. Survival. Survival was what mattered, and in order to survive the box would have to go. They needed the money, and they needed a plan.

Gia had neither, but could get both. And so, she would. They would be fine. She walked to Gavin, kneeling down in the dirt next to him and brushing a piece of hair from his face. "Gav?" she whispered. "Wake up."

He stirred. "What is it?" He looked around in confusion before he seemed to realize where they were.

"We've got to get moving." She looked over her shoulder. "Before anyone comes through here and catches us."

"Where are we going?" he asked.

"Anywhere," she promised. "Everywhere. Far from here." She tried to make it sound like an adventure. "As long as we're together, it doesn't matter where we are, right?"

He smiled, rubbing his hands through her hair playfully. "Whatever you say, sappy."

She locked arms with him as he stood up, and a smile filled her face. "What's that look about?" he asked, staring at her.

"We're free," she said softly, looking up to the sky. "I think I'm finally starting to realize that."

"Free? What were we before?"

"We were prisoners, Gav."

He seemed to think about it for a moment before looking to the sky. "We broke the chains!" he bellowed into the quiet air around them.

"Gavin! Someone will hear you!" She tried to silence him.

He looked around, holding his hands up. "No one is here, Gia. Just scream it. Let it out. You'll feel better."

She contemplated, feeling unsure.

"Go on," he urged her. "Just scream. It's what a free woman would do."

She looked to the sky, opening her mouth and screaming into the open sky, her voice echoing loudly as she felt the chains that had weighed her down finally breaking free. And then, when she'd finished, she began to run.

TWENTY-EIGHT

FIONA

Fiona woke up on the couch, Logan's arms wrapped around her still. She rolled over, wincing from pain. He stirred, leaning back and smiling at her sleepily. He kissed her forehead. "Good morning," he said.

She looked up, surprised to see that the room was still empty. "Good morning," she told him, attempting to sit up.

"Wait, wait," he cautioned her, climbing off the couch and helping her up slowly. She rolled her eyes playfully, though she let him help her to stand. "Where to?"

"Uh, I have to pee," she said. "And you are not helping me with that."

He smirked. "Fair enough. I'll help you down the hall, though."

They began hobbling toward the bathroom, all of Fiona's weight resting on Logan. She groaned, feeling entirely helpless, but continued on. They arrived in front of the bathroom, and Logan stopped, pushing the door open. "Do you need me to help you?"

"No," she said firmly, easing into the room and shutting the door. She sat on the toilet carefully, trying her hardest to keep her leg straight. When she was finished, she stood up, hopping to the sink and washing her hands. She looked in the mirror, shocked by her haggard appearance. How in the world was this guy not running for the hills at the mere sight of her? She ran her hands under the water again, splashing it onto her face. She brushed her fingers through her hair, trying to tame the tangles somewhat. It wasn't much better, honestly, but it was something. She turned back around, holding on to the wall as she made her way toward the door and swung it open. Logan and Fletcher were standing against the wall, staring around awkwardly.

"Good morning," Fletcher said, nodding to her.

"Good morning."

Logan took her arm, helping her to get steady before making their way back down the hall as Fletcher walked into the bathroom. He sat her down on the couch, adjusting the pillows behind her.

"I'm fine," she said, though she was smiling. It felt good, yet completely foreign, to have someone taking care of her.

He nodded. "I know you are. It doesn't hurt to have me help you though."

She squeezed his hand. "You're right. Thank you. I'm sorry, I'm just...I'm not used to this."

"To what?"

"To people caring about me."

He swallowed, his gaze faltering. "Well," he said, face serious, "get used to it."

The front door to the house opened unexpectedly, causing the couple to jump. Fiona looked to the door, where a cola-haired woman stood. She wore thick eyeliner and a tight, leopard print sweater over her coal black pants. She was carrying a toddler, her tiny, blonde head resting on the woman's shoulder.

"Oh, hello," she said softly. "I didn't realize there'd be company."

"Who are you?" Fiona asked, scooting to the edge of the couch, prepared to run or attack, whichever was necessary.

"I'm—"

"Nova," Quinn's voice called from behind them. "Hi, baby," she cooed, pulling the child into her arms. The girl immediately began fussing, and Quinn bounced as she talked. "I thought you weren't going to be back until tomorrow."

"We got home early," she said. "I didn't realize you'd have people here. Do you need me to keep her?"

"No," Quinn answered, though she didn't look entirely convinced. "It'll be fine." She looked to Fiona. "I'm sorry. I'm being rude, I guess. Nova, this is...erm, Fiona. Fiona...I'm sorry, I can't remember your last name."

"Denali," Fiona told her.

"Right, Denali. Fiona, this is Nova Phillips. She's, um...a friend of the family?" She let out a laugh. "God, my life is complicated."

Nova nodded toward her. "It's great to meet you, Fiona."

"She's staying with us for a while."

"Looks like you've got a whole crew staying with you," she said, pointing to the full driveway.

"You remember Gunner, right? Jesse's...I don't know what he is. Ex-fiancée's husband?"

"Rick's son?" Nova asked. "Your—"

"Yep, him," Quinn answered quickly. "He needed a place to stay for a while. Fiona and Fletcher are his...cousins. And, they're all staying here."

"Oh," Nova said, obviously confused. "Okay."

The bathroom door opened, and Fletcher walked out, headed down the short hallway. When he entered the living room, Nova let out a sharp gasp.

"What?" Quinn asked.

Nova stared at him a moment too long. "Nothing, it's just...you look just like him."

"Who?" Fletcher asked.

"Rick," she answered. "You're his...nephew?"

"Um, sure?" Fletcher said, scratching his head. "I'm sorry, who are you?"

"I'm Nova. I was...I mean, Rick was...he was really special to me," she said softly. "I was so sorry to hear he'd passed."

"Right," Fletcher cleared his throat. "Thanks."

"Anyway, I should be going," Nova said, but stopped as Gunner walked into the room. "You must be Gunner."

He nodded at her, his hair messy from sleep. "And you are?"

"I'm Nova. I was a friend of your father." She smiled. "I said your cousin looked like him...but you are the spitting image." She cocked her head to the side, staring at him strangely. Finally, she looked away, her head down. "I'm sorry. It's just...it's hard to see him, to see you, after all this time." She closed her eyes, letting out a soft laugh. "I'm sorry. You must think I'm crazy."

Quinn put a protective hand over her shoulder. "Are you okay?"

Nova nodded. "I'll be fine," she said. "Just surprised."

"You were in love with him," Logan's voice carried across the room, shocking everyone.

"What?" Fiona asked.

Logan's eyes never left Nova, though he spoke to Fiona. "She was in love with Gunner's father."

Nova shook her head. "I'm sorry...what are you talking about?"

"Is it true?" Gunner asked, staring at her. "Are you the woman he had an affair with?"

Quinn tensed. "You knew?"

Gunner looked at her. "Wait, *you* knew?"

Fletcher looked around. "Can someone please tell me what in the hell is going on?"

Just then someone knocked on the door. Quinn moved to answer the door and, at the same time, Logan spoke. "Yeah, I think he can."

The door opened, and everyone in the room gasped. His gray eyes fell on Fiona, and she spoke the only word she could muster. "Dad?"

TWENTY-NINE

FIONA

Fiona stared into her father's face, confusion, grief, and anger filling her equally.

Gunner and Fletcher stared at him, neither one speaking. The room was eerily still as everyone watched the last man anyone had expected to walk into the room.

"Hi," he said finally, clearing his throat. He had aged significantly since they'd last seen him, his body more full, his hair more thin. He carried heavy wrinkles around his eyes and laugh lines he'd had no cause for before.

"Hi?" Gunner asked, his voice filled with anger. He sat down, still staring. Fletcher remained standing, though he looked like he might pass out. Nova had gone ghost white, her eyes blinking rapidly.

"Rick?" she said finally. "It's...it's really you?" She took Quinn's hand, who looked completely terrified. She stepped behind Nova, as if protecting the child in her arms.

"It's really me," he said. "I...I know I owe you all an explanation."

"A lot fucking more than that," Fiona spat, attempting to stand up.

"How did you find us?" Fletcher asked. Everyone seemed to want to know the answer to that. Rick looked to Fiona and then to Logan beside her. He bowed his head in his direction. Fiona turned to him.

"You knew my father?" she demanded.

"Yes," he answered quietly.

"He was the man who called you? The one I talked to?"

"FD. Fiona's dad," he answered.

She pushed up from the couch, ignoring the pain and moving across the room, trying to head for the door. "Wait, Fi," Fletcher said, but Fiona held her hand up to stop him.

"Leave me alone," she cried. "All of you." She began to fall as she approached the door, and Rick caught her. She struggled against his weight, punching and clawing at his chest as her sobs tore through the room. "How could you?" she demanded. "I trusted you. I waited for you." More punches. "I needed you."

He waited until her punches slowed, allowing her to work through all of her rage before he wrapped his arms around her. "I'm sorry, my Gia. I'm so sorry for everything. I can explain it all. I will explain it all. But it won't be enough for you to forgive me."

She slammed her hands into his chest again. "I hate you," she said angrily. "I hate you." She opened her mouth, wanting to say more. Wanting to tell him what she'd gone through because of him. Wanting to tell him what she'd lost —what they'd all lost. But no words would form. Instead, her body shook with tears, all power in her gone. She sank to the floor, and Fletcher and Logan were at her side in an instant.

"I want answers, now," Gunner demanded from where he was standing again. "I wanna know what happened. Where in the hell you've been and why you're here now." He looked at Logan. "And then I want to know why you told our father where to find us, because none of us wanted to be found. So, after we get all of that, you can both leave. What you've done," he said to Logan, "tricking Fiona the way you have...you have no idea what this family is capable of."

"I didn't trick her," he said, holding his hands up. "I was trying to help her. I was trying to help all of you."

"How?" Fiona asked, anger still pulsing in her veins. "You lied to me, Logan. You lied to me about everything."

"I never lied to you. I told you everything you asked. I told you I was searching for you. I told you I'd explain who the man was on the phone when I got the chance. I wanted to do it the right way."

"And this is the right way?" Quinn asked. "By springing their abusive father at them? By giving him my address so he can come here and hurt my children?"

"What?" Logan asked, looking to Rick and back to Fiona. "Abusive? Is that true?"

"Yes," Quinn answered.

"No," Fiona and Fletcher said at once.

"No?" Quinn asked.

Just then, Jesse, Vaida, Nora, and Reagan walked into the room. Reagan carried their youngest child close to her chest. "What's going on?" she asked, her eyes landing on Rick then back on Gunner.

Jesse hurried to Quinn. "Who is this?"

"This is Rick James," she said to him, her eyes never leaving Rick, her grip tight around the child. Jesse stepped forward.

"Rick James...as in...?" he asked, his eyes wide.

"The very one," Quinn answered.

"I thought he was dead. What in the hell is going on?" Jesse asked.

"I think that's what we'd all like to know," Gunner answered.

Rick sighed. "I'm happy to tell you everything," he said, "but I need you all to hear me out."

They remained still, everyone on high alert as Rick began to tell his story.

THIRTY

RICK
THE NIGHT OF THE FIRE

When his daughter disappeared through the doorway, he stared at the glass in his hand. The glass he was supposed to pour down the drain. To pretend to drink for Misty's sake so that he could escape while she thought he was passed out.

His throat was dry, his mind tempting him to take a drink of the only band aid that had ever worked. He didn't need a band-aid, he reminded himself. He wasn't the monster he'd believed himself to be. He wasn't evil. He was going to save his children. He was going to protect them from the true monster.

He tried to replay the thoughts over and over, tried to find the strength to toss the drink out like he'd promised to, but he couldn't. In the end, his addiction won. He needed it. He craved the burn. And so, knowing what it would mean for his children, he took the drink anyway. Alcohol always won.

When the time came, he was beginning to get groggy, but he was still awake. He lit the lighter fluid-covered cloth with his lighter, burning his hand but unable to feel the singe. He walked to the window—stumbled, more realistically—and climbed out. He walked through the field. He had promised Gia he'd get a car, but he couldn't remember where he was planning to get it from. He couldn't remember much. And then, he couldn't remember why any of it mattered. As he hit the edge of the woods opposite where Gia and Gavin would be waiting, a mile from where he'd promised to meet them, the familiar wave of black found him, and he welcomed it like an old friend.

THE NEXT DAY, *Rick woke up, his head pounding. He could smell smoke instantly and remembered what he had done. He sat up, looking at the gray smoke that still billowed into the sky. He wondered about his children and tried to remember which direction he'd told them to head.*

He considered going to them, even headed to where he hoped they'd still be waiting, but stopped himself before he reached them. His head was bleeding from the fall, his hands shaking, and he was a complete wreck. And yet, already he was thinking of alcohol. Of when he'd have access to his next drink.

He was going to be no use to his children. He knew that, though it destroyed him to admit it. If anything, he was going to be more of a burden. He couldn't save them. He couldn't help them when the only thoughts that consumed his mind were those filled with whiskey. He'd become his father, and his father's father, and probably even further back than that. His fate was one laid out for him before he was even born, and he'd succumb to it so easily.

And so, with tears in his eyes, but drink on his mind, he turned. He walked away from his children when they needed him most. He walked away and promised to make them proud. To get himself clean and then to find them someday. But first, he needed a drink.

THIRTY-ONE

RICK
THREE MONTHS AGO

Rick sat at the coffee shop across from Terry. They were in their usual spot, with their usual half-empty cups of coffee.

"Did you make a meeting last week?" Terry asked, making his sponsor duties a priority, like always.

"Yep," Rick said, taking another drink. "You?"

"You know I did," Terry told him.

"How are you doing?"

Terry nodded, though his watery eyes told a different story. "I'm...I'm still sober," he said. "That's about all I can say."

"Have they caught the prick who did it?"

Terry shook his head. "Nope. Not yet. Her boss is missing, too. They're thinking he may have been killed trying to escape."

"Damn nonsense. Can't even go to work anymore without having to worry about getting gunned down."

Terry wiped his eyes quickly, though the tears continued to fall. "I just keep thinking...she had so much to live for. She was getting married next fall. She was planning to go back to medical school to get her degree. She loved what she did. Loved everything about helping people. That's who my Madeline was. The most compassionate woman I'd ever known."

Rick took another drink. He'd always been uncomfortable with grief, though he'd known his fair share of it. "They'll catch him, Terry. They'll get justice for your daughter."

"Justice won't bring her back," he cried. "I just want her back."

"I know," Rick said, not knowing what else to say. "I know."

Terry cleared his throat, taking another drink, his jaw still shaking. "Have you gotten in contact with your children yet?"

"No," Rick said. "I wouldn't know the first place to start. They're better off without me anyway. Always have been."

"I'll let you in on a little secret," Terry whispered, reaching in his pocket. "I've got a private investigator searching for Madeline's killer. He's...unconventional, but efficient. He came highly recommended by a friend of mine who caught his wife cheating. Not really the same thing, but he's good." He handed over a white business card. "He could find your kids. Help you get into contact with them."

Rick stared at the card, shaking his head. "I don't know, man."

Terry took his hand, squeezing it tight. "Trust me, Rick, you don't want to wait and lose your chance. If I could have just one more day with my Maddy, I would. You're wasting your children's whole lives."

"They'll never forgive me for what I did." He ran his fingers over the lettering on the white card.

"Maybe not. But it's better to know that for sure, after you've tried to fix it, than to always wonder."

Rick took the last drink of his coffee, sliding out from the booth. "I'll think about it, okay?" he asked, tapping the card and slipping it into his pocket.

"Okay," he said calmly.

"You take care of yourself," Rick told his friend, patting his shoulder.

"You too, Rick. I'll see you next week."

He nodded. "You call if you need me sooner. We'll go to a meeting together."

Terry nodded, downing the last of his coffee and turning from him. "Will do."

Rick headed out of the diner, walking out onto the quiet street. Woodward, Oklahoma had become a nice home for him. It was quiet, the people were friendly, and he'd found his place. But, no matter how hard he'd tried to forget his past, his children were always on his mind. It had taken him three years to decide to get clean and another year to finally feel like it was working. He'd met Terry around that time and gotten to know a few other men from their AA meetings.

He'd gotten a house, a small rental property, and a job at a local mechanic shop. He'd gone by his first name, though he claimed his last name was Jameson. Close enough for him to remember when he was drunk. He stopped at the trash can, contemplating the card once more. What could it hurt? He could at least call.

He opened his small flip phone, dialing the number and pressing the phone to his ear.

The line rang once. "SOS Security," the man's gruff voice came over the line. "This is Frank."

"Hey, Frank. My name is Rick...Rick Jameson. A friend of mine gave me this number. I wondered if I could meet with you. I may have a case."

"Sure thing. Where you located, bud?"

"I'm in Woodward."

"Oklahoma? The place with the shooting?"

"Yeah, my friend Terry hired you to investigate his daughter's death."

"Gotcha. Okay, I'm in St. Louis today, but I'll tell you what. Can we meet tomorrow?"

"Okay," Rick said.

Frank gave him directions to the place they would meet, and Rick scrawled them down on his calloused palm. "Okay, see you soon."

"See you soon," he agreed.

THIRTY-TWO

RICK
TWO MONTHS AGO

Rick sat across from Frank, staring intently at the file in his hands. "Did you find them?"

Frank nodded slowly. "Yeah, I think I did."

Rick's eyes widened. "I'm impressed."

"I'm damn good at my job," Frank said cockily. "Now," he pulled three pictures out and laid them down, "don't get too disappointed if I'm wrong. We can try again." Rick nodded and Frank turned over the first picture. "Do you recognize him?"

Rick picked up the picture of Gunner, running a finger over his son's face. He was at the park, a little dark-haired girl's fingers laced through his. He looked happy. Rick felt his eyes watering immediately, feeling embarrassed. "That's Gunner."

Frank nodded. "I was fairly certain about him. He's using

the same name and living back in the town you were from: Dale, Georgia." He watched Rick's expression before he went on. "The other two were more tricky. I didn't find anything about Gia or Gavin James, other than the fact that they died years ago. I looked into a few others; James isn't too uncommon of a last name, so there was a good chance I'd be chasing my tail trying to find them that way. So, instead, I looked for connections to Gunner. He is married to a Reagan Orrick. Do you know her?"

Rick nodded. "I did. She dated Gunner in high school."

Frank smiled. "There. I love a happy ending." His face went serious again. "But, unfortunately Reagan Orrick's little sister, Holly, didn't have such a happy ending. She was found dead in an apartment that was...get this, next door to an apartment Gunner had rented. Coincidence? I don't believe in 'em. So, I looked into the circumstances surrounding her death. The man who called nine-one-one, the man who later signed off on her apartment cleaning bill, his name was Fletcher Denali. Heard of him?"

"No," Rick answered.

"Well, I didn't assume you would. See, Fletcher Denali died several years ago. So, how is it possible that just two years ago, he was paying for a biodecontamination specialist to clean up Holly Orrick's death?"

"I don't follow."

Frank turned over the second photo. One of a dark-haired man in a diner uniform. He stood with his arm around a short, balding man. Rick picked up the photo, looking closer, his throat tight. "It's Gavin."

Frank nodded. "Ah, good. That will make this next one much easier. Now, I'm afraid I haven't been able to track down his current whereabouts. I do know that he lived in Atlanta when this was taken. I was able to track down a diner where I thought he might be, and I pulled this picture from their Facebook page. He was foolish enough to let them post his name, but lucky for us, because it made our job much easier. I'm sure he just assumed no one would be looking for him under his alias."

Rick nodded. "But, you think you can find him? Gia will be with him."

"I don't know that she is," Frank said. "This next one is the kind of news I don't necessarily love to give. When I did a database search for Fletcher Denali, I came across some receipts for a private payment to a Rose Acres. It's a psychiatric facility in Atlanta, Georgia."

Rick took a sharp breath, shaking his head. "Gavin is in a psychiatric facility? Could it be addiction?" He thought back to his own past, worrying he'd passed on the ugliest parts of himself to his son. No, not possible. Gavin wasn't his son. Except that he was, in every way that mattered.

"I don't know what it is," he answered honestly. "I couldn't say. But I don't think it's Fletcher that's there. The payment was made for a Fiona Denali. This is the photo I pulled from her intake paperwork." He flipped the last picture over, and Rick stared at it without picking it up.

The photo was Gia, there was no doubt. Her dark hair had been died a murky blonde, her roots grown out. Her eyes were dark, the skin around them sunken in, her gaze glassy. If he hadn't known better, he'd have believed she was dead.

"Oh," he said, moving the picture toward him with shaking hands. What had he done? What had he let her become? He stared at the picture of his daughter who was now

no more than a stranger. "Oh no." He couldn't hold back his tears then, his sorrow overwhelming. "I have to go to her. I have to find her."

Frank held a hand out as Rick went to stand. "Wait. There's more. You're going to have a hard time tracking her. She's no longer at the facility. It shows she was discharged a few days ago."

"So, she'll be with Fletcher then, right?"

"I don't know. I haven't been able to find anything else on Fletcher at all. I'm sorry," he said. "But, I do have one more thing that may help. Your wife passed away four months ago. Did you know that?"

Rick shook his head. "I didn't." Not that he wanted to know. He couldn't get his children's faces out of his head, the horror that must haunt them all.

"She had cancer. The week that you hired me, I sent someone from my team to tail Gunner, since he was the easiest for me to track down. And he did manage to see a man and woman visiting Gunner, a couple who weren't regular visitors. We got pictures, but they're difficult to make out. You can't tell for certain, but the man might have been Gavin. For the past six weeks, we have watched Gunner's home, but the man has not returned." He paused. "However, a young woman did visit. She didn't stay, didn't even knock on the door, in fact, but she did tape something on the door. We managed to capture this photo of her." He pulled a photo from the folder, turning it over. "It's not great either, but I do think it's her."

Rick held the grainy, zoomed in picture to his face, trying to decide if it might be her. "I got ahold of the plate number and have my team watching traffic cams to search her route.

When we can pinpoint where she might be headed, I can give that information to you. I think your best option at this point is to get in contact with Gunner and see if he can lead you to the others."

"No," he said firmly, staring at Gunner's photo. "He looks happy. He doesn't need me." He touched Gia's photo. "She needs me."

Frank sighed. "Okay. But, you should be aware that if she is unstable...which is likely, based on the history you gave me and her medical records I was able to access, you're going to want someone professional to handle her. I don't think it's a good idea for you to go alone. But, I can't stop you, either."

"Thank you. I'll keep that in mind," Rick said. "Can I take this?"

"It's all yours," he agreed. "Take whatever you want. I'll be in touch as soon as I get a hit on Gia's plate. My team's pretty thorough. It shouldn't take long." He held out a hand to shake Rick's.

"I can't thank you enough. I never thought this was possible." He paused before walking away. "Hey, I wanted to ask, my friend Terry...you were searching for his daughter's killer. Did you find him yet? Terry's...well, he's not doing well. I haven't seen him in a while."

"No," Frank said. "I'm not really supposed to talk about other cases, but we're working hard to find him. It's just not happening as fast as we'd like."

"And her boss? No word on him, either?"

Frank lowered his brow. "The doctor? We've found him. He's safe." He gave a quick nod.

"Good," Rick said. "That's good. Madeline always liked

him." Just then, he got an idea. "Hey, he must be out of work, huh?"

"What? Work? Yeah, I'm sure he is."

He raised his brow, suddenly full of hope. "You think he'd be up for a job?"

THIRTY-THREE

RICK
ONE MONTH AGO

A month later, Frank contacted Rick with the direction he believed Gia was heading. He also gave him a number for Logan, though he would give him nothing else. "I shouldn't even be giving you this," he warned. "But, like I said, I like seeing happy endings."

Rick hung up the phone and dialed the number. It went to voicemail after one ring, but he dialed again instantly and the line was picked up.

"Hello?" an unsure voice on the other line asked.

"Is this Dr. Logan North?"

"Who's asking?"

"Please don't hang up," Rick said. "Please. I need your help."

"Help with what? Who is this?"

Rick paced as he talked, his voice shaking. "It's my daughter," he said. "She's very sick. She needs a doctor."

"Is this a prank?"

"No," Rick said, "of course not. I know what happened to you. I know about the shooting. My friend's daughter was Madeline, the, um—"

"I know who Madeline is. So does everyone who has watched the news over the past few months. What do you want?"

"I told you, I need your help with my daughter."

"I'm not exactly in a position to help anyone."

"That's exactly why you're perfect to help her. She needs someone who's...um, down on his luck. Like she is."

"Down on his luck?" He laughed. "Yeah, I guess you could say that. Look, I don't have an office or a way to see patients. And, even if I did, I'm not safe to be around right now. The shooter is still searching for me. And I'm on a month-long diet of nothing but alcohol, so I'm guessing there are about a million different doctors out there who could do better for your daughter. I'm sorry, I just can't do it. I'd be no use to you."

"I've been where you are," he whispered, recognizing the hopelessness in his voice.

"What?"

"Drowning myself in alcohol to compensate for my shit life," he said. "It doesn't make it better. It doesn't help anything. In fact, it's the reason my daughter is suffering. It's the reason so many people have suffered. Whatever you're going through, alcohol isn't going to help."

"Gee, thanks a lot, Dad."

"You know, I have three kids. Almost had four. But, I

haven't heard anyone call me that in years. And I'm the only one to blame. And you're the only person who I believe might be able to help me. Who knows? It might help you just as much."

Logan groaned, and Rick heard him taking another drink. "Who knows?" He feigned excitement. "But then again, it might not. If you want a happy ending, old man, turn on the Hallmark Channel." With that, the line went dead, and Rick tossed his phone across the room. Now what was he going to do?

THE NEXT DAY, *his phone rang. He recognized Logan's number instantly, answering it as fast as his hands would move.*

"Hello?" he called before the phone even made it to his ear.

"How much does the job pay?"

"How much do you need?" Rick asked, staring at the jar of cash on his counter. It wasn't much.

"Well, what am I going to be doing?"

"Are you saying you're in?"

"Don't get ahead of ourselves," Logan said quickly. "I'm saying I'll hear you out. I could use the cash."

Tears filled Rick's eyes again, knowing he was going to see his daughter again. Knowing somehow, someway, everything was going to work out.

THIRTY-FOUR

FIONA

Fiona listened to her father's story in its entirety. She let him explain why he chose not to come after her, about how much he'd missed them all, and about how much he'd done to try to find them. He explained how he set it all up, arranged for Logan to meet her at the gas station, and how they'd been in contact since then, with the end game being that Logan would ease her into considering seeing her father again.

Every word felt like betrayal. How was she just supposed to accept this? Once again, the person she'd chosen to trust had lied to her. Even if he never meant to hurt her, the way they had met had been planned. He had lied about not knowing anything about who she was. He had known the secret that could have changed her life. She hadn't killed her father. The burden she'd carried for so many years was never hers to carry. So, why didn't she feel better?

"I couldn't come with you, sweetheart," Rick said again. "You have no idea how badly I wanted to. I was of no use to you."

"We managed," Fiona said firmly, running her fingers over her thighs nervously.

"So, you've been alive all these years...just out there somewhere knowing your daughter was living with the guilt of killing you?" Fletcher asked, then looked at Fiona. "And you, why didn't you tell me? Why wouldn't you let me share that pain with you?"

"It wasn't your pain to carry, Fletcher. It never was. I made the decisions. I'm the one who started the fire. I'm the one who killed Holly. I'm the one who tried to kill you," she looked to Reagan, "and there's no excuse. There's not. I...whatever was wrong with Mom...it's wrong with me, too. My head is screwed up. But, I don't want to hurt you. None of you."

Reagan's face was stone-still and she didn't respond. Rick looked as though he were going to be sick. "You killed people, Gia?"

"I'm Fiona," she snapped. "I will never *ever* be Gia again. Gia was weak. I am not."

Rick pulled her into a hug despite her feral stance, and Fiona relaxed slightly in his arms. She felt safe somehow, though it was a strange safeness. "Fiona, then. I'm so sorry for whatever you've had to do. Whatever you've had to live through. I love you so much, my sweet girl. I always have."

She pulled away. "You don't abandon the people you love." She looked up to Fletcher and Gunner.

Fletcher lowered his brow at her. "I didn't abandon you, Fiona. I wouldn't. We've talked about this."

"Look, I know I can't make up for all of this within an hour long conversation. I know I have years of pain to make up for. But, I do hope this can be a starting point to get us to somewhere better than this. I'm not expecting anything. If you want me to leave...I'll respect that. But I wanted you to know, I do love you. And despite everything, I am your father. I was a lousy one before, and there's a good chance I'll never be a great one. But, I'm clean now. Sober six years. I have a job and a house. I take care of myself. I pay my bills. I've worked hard to get myself where I am, but I know that still doesn't make anything you kids have gone through all right. I know that what your mother did to you, it's unforgivable, and I know that I will always have a role in that. I'm not blameless. But, I never hurt you on purpose." He shook his head. "You may not believe that, but it's the god's honest truth. I loved you with all of my heart. I made mistakes." He looked at Nova. "I made so many mistakes. But, I'm here now. I want to make it up to you." His gaze danced around the room. "To all of you." He cleared his throat. "If you'll give me the chance."

The room was silent, everyone waiting for each person to speak, but no one did. Finally, Rick's shoulders fell. He reached in his pocket and pulled out a stack of cash, holding it out for Logan. "The rest of my bill." Logan took it cautiously, looking at Fiona, though she wouldn't look his way. "I'll be going." He waved over his shoulder, small tears in his eyes. "You'll take care of each other, right?"

"We always have," Gunner said, putting a hand on Fletcher's shoulder.

"Right," Rick said, turning and shutting the door behind him as he disappeared.

The room was silent, Gunner, Fiona, and Fletcher each looking at each other. Their faces were unreadable.

Finally, Nova spoke up. "I'm sorry. I'm so sorry. I can't let him leave like that."

THIRTY-FIVE

NOVA

Nova rushed forward, swinging open the door and hurrying out. She rushed down the porch. Rick James had been the love of her life once. He'd also been the heartache of her life, but it all felt like a dream to be seeing him again. Like the second chance she never thought she could have. "Rick!" He turned around upon hearing his name.

"Nova?" He accepted her hug as she catapulted into his arms. "I can't believe it's you."

"I know. I never thought I'd see you again." Tears were in her eyes as she was surrounded by the arms of the only man she'd ever loved. "I know I'm supposed to hate you, and I know I shouldn't do this, but I thought you were dead. I thought you were gone." She squeezed him tighter, his chin resting on her head.

"I know," he said, rubbing her back. "I can't believe you're here. What on earth are you doing with my kids?"

"Well," she said, looking up at him, though she didn't completely release him. "I'm here with mine."

"Yours?" His face fell. "You have a child? That's...that's great. Congratulations." She could tell he didn't mean it, though he was trying hard to pretend. "We have so much to catch up on."

"Yes," she said. "We do." She wiped a tear from her eyes, smearing her mascara but not caring in the slightest. "Because the child I'm here with...she isn't just mine, Rick. She's yours."

THIRTY-SIX

RICK
THIRTY YEARS AGO

"Misty, I know this isn't what you want to hear, but I'm in love with someone else." He shook his head. "Misty, I can't take the fighting anymore. I'm moving out." Still not right. "Misty, I've fallen in love with Novalee Phillips. She's pregnant, and I want a divorce." Still not right. He slammed a fist into the wall, searching for the right way to tell his wife the news. Nothing would work. No matter what, the night would end in a fight. Gunner would be screaming, and it would make it all worse.

Rick took a drink of his beer. He had to do it. It was like a Band-Aid. He would wait until Gunner had been put down for the night, and then he would just rip it off. It had to be done. Sad as it was, he didn't love Misty anymore. Hadn't in so long. Novalee was kind to him, she didn't try to manipulate him. It hadn't been intentional, and this baby certainly wasn't planned, but he couldn't deny how much he wanted a family with Novalee. Maybe Misty would agree to joint custody of Gunner. Lord knows it was Rick doing everything with him anyway.

But Misty wouldn't give in. That was just how she was. It had very little to do with actually caring about Gunner, or Rick for that matter, and quite a lot to do with winning. Winning was everything to his wife. But she wouldn't win this.

Rick was tired of losing.

THAT NIGHT, *Gunner had been put down, and Rick was washing dishes. Misty walked into the room, shoving past him to get herself a pain pill.*

"Headache?" he asked.

"Yes," she mumbled. "Like always."

He turned off the water. "Misty, can we talk?"

She tossed the pill in her mouth, taking a gulp of wine. "Sure." She didn't bother to look his way.

"It's...um, well," he took a breath, reminding himself to be assertive, "I need to tell you something. You aren't going to like it, but it needs to be said."

"What?" She was looking at him now.

"I've fallen in love with someone else."

She laughed. "Oh you have, have you?"

"Yes," he said. "She's pregnant. I'm sorry, Misty, but I'm leaving you."

She stared at him, her eyes narrowing in his direction.

Finally, without warning, she launched the wine glass at his head. "Who is she?"

He shook his head. "It doesn't matter."

"You're wrong about that," she spat. "It damn well will matter when I find out who she is."

"You're going to leave her alone, Misty. I'll be fair in the divorce. Joint custody of Gunner. I'll pay you alimony. Whatever you want. But, I'm not going to change my mind about this. I'm not happy anymore. You can't be either. All we ever do is fight."

Misty walked to the counter, pulling out a knife. "You want joint custody, huh?"

"Misty, what are you doing?"

She walked down the hall, her hips swaying as she twirled the knife slowly in the air. "What joint do you want, Rick? A finger? A toe?" She pushed open the door to Gunner's bedroom.

"Misty, stop it. Stop it, please!" He tried to keep his voice low, though it didn't matter. Misty walked to the crib, jerking the child up quickly. She held the knife up with her free hand.

"I said what joint, Rick?"

He watched in horror as Gunner began screaming, Misty seeming completely oblivious to it. "No, stop. Please. I'll do whatever you want. Please. I'll never see her again. I won't."

"And the baby?" she asked, an evil smirk on her face. Gunner continued screaming, though she'd lowered the knife and was holding him closer. He kept his eyes on it, the sharp edge still just inches from his child.

"There is no baby." He shook his head. "There won't be a baby."

She nodded. "Good." Leaning over the crib, she laid

Gunner down, turning and walking from the room without a word. When she'd gone, Rick rushed to his son, picking him up and cradling next to his chest. He kissed his head, tears releasing as his adrenaline calmed.

"I'm so sorry, Gunner," he whispered. And he was. He was sorry about everything. Would Misty have actually hurt their child? He couldn't be sure. But, he couldn't risk it. He could never risk it again.

THIRTY-SEVEN

RICK

"What do you mean?" he asked, staring into her dark eyes. "My child? You lost our child..."

"No," she said, shaking her head. "Our child is Quinn." Her smile was sad. "And she's perfect, Rick. She's amazing. Beautiful and smart and...she reminds me so much of you. She has your kindness." She bumped his hip with hers playfully. "And my good looks."

He furrowed his brow. "I don't understand. They told me you'd lost the baby."

She took his hand. "It's a very long story. One I'll explain to you someday. For now, I just want to hold you."

He leaned down, his lips moving for hers, but he stopped. "I'm sorry," he whispered. "It's habit." He wanted so badly to kiss her again. Even just once.

"You don't have to apologize," she said.

"I do. I really, really do. Part of AA is that we have to make amends to the people we've hurt. And, after my children, you're at the top of that list." He shook his head, his heart hurting. How could so much joy and heartbreak be packed into one day? "I never should've left you, Nova. I never should've left you alone. I know you didn't have anyone else. I know what my decision did to you. I didn't have a choice. I honestly didn't, but that's no excuse. I tried to do the right thing, but no matter what, someone got hurt. And that someone was you. And my children. It was always the person who didn't deserve to be hurt. I should've never stayed with Misty. I could explain all the reasons that I did, but most of them wouldn't make any sense. All I can tell you is that I've spent every day since I walked away from you that night just dreaming of what could've been. Just dreaming of this moment and all the things I'd say to you."

"Oh, yeah?" she asked, staring at him with wide eyes. "What sort of things?"

"Crazy things," he told her. "Messy things. Things like...how I never stopped loving you."

"I never stopped loving you either," she admitted, surprising him. "I know I should be playing hard to get. I really do. But I can't, Rick. I know our past is messy. I know that everything we've gone through should've destroyed us...but *I never thought I'd see you again.*" More tears formed in her eyes. "And so none of the rest of that seems to matter."

He leaned down, his lips on hers, finding the familiar comfort he'd once loved. Still loved. He could feel it, the warmth and love he'd always had for her. It was there in his chest, rising and falling with each breath. It had never truly gone away. He cupped her cheeks, his thumbs rubbing away tears as their kiss grew. It was heartbreaking and complicated, yet beautiful and perfect all at once. And he was home, perfectly at home, right there in her arms. It was what he'd been looking for all along.

THIRTY-EIGHT

FIONA

Fiona hobbled out onto the porch without anyone's help. She sat on the porch swing, watching Rick and Nova in the driveway. She rolled her eyes. That was a different problem for a different day.

Logan opened the door, walking out. "Do you mind if I join you?"

She shook her head without looking at him. "Can't stop you."

He leaned against the porch rail in front of her. "I know you're mad."

"Gee, Doc, what makes you think that?"

He brushed a piece of hair from his face. "Fiona, look, you have every right to be pissed at me. You do. Maybe I handled things the wrong way, I don't know. What I do know is that I never intended to care. When your father contacted me, it was to do a job. I couldn't use my cards, and I only had so much cash saved up. I could use whatever extra money I could get. I'm not going to lie to you, I thought this would be an easy job. Meet you, introduce you to your father, provide him with a diagnosis. The end. But that wasn't the case. When we met, I was a mess. I was suicidal, depressed, lethargic. I didn't see a point in going on." He paused. "You gave me a reason to keep moving, Fiona, to keep living. You are the reason I'm still here. I couldn't care less about the money now."

"It's not about the money, Logan."

"Then what is it about?"

"You lied to me."

"What, because you were so open with me about your past?" he asked. "I didn't lie to you, Fiona. I didn't tell you things, sure, but when you asked me direct questions, I was always honest with you. I was completing a job...but I was also falling for the assignment."

She felt her face grow warm, looking down. He moved to sit beside her, sliding a finger under her chin and lifting it so she would look at him. "I know the way we started is complicated, Fiona. I know nothing about our relationship is ideal. But, I do care about you. I really do. And I think you could learn to care about me someday. If you gave yourself the chance."

She nodded. "I don't know how to do that anymore, Logan. I don't know how to let people in and just blindly trust them."

"I'm not asking you to blindly trust me. I'm asking you to let me earn your trust."

"What if I can never trust you? What if something in me is broken and I just...can't?"

"You aren't broken, Fiona. But, even if you are, I can handle it. I can handle whatever you throw at me. More than that, I want to. I want to help you...and I want you to help me, too."

"How can I help you?"

"By showing me the good things in life again. The things I had almost forgotten about."

"Like what?" she asked, raising a brow. What good could she possibly have to offer—he interrupted her thoughts with a kiss, his lips square on hers. It was tender, his thumb on her jawbone, and it ended in a flash, before she was ready.

"Like that," he said. "Like kissing the girl I'm falling in love with, or sitting in front of our fireplace with a glass of wine at the end of a long day. Like cooking a meal together or watching a show on the couch. Planning a future together. Believing in that future. All the big things but all the little things, too. Because it's all beautiful, Fiona. It all fits and meshes—the good and the bad, the big and the small—and it builds this amazing life. And I think it's time that we start living it."

She patted his cheek and pressed her lips to his carefully. "You're a dreamer." A small smile formed on her lips. "But that life will never be mine. I don't get simple meals together or drinking a glass of wine. My life is survival. Constantly watching over my shoulder. Never settling in one place for too long."

"Why?" he asked. "It's like I told you...we're free, Fiona. Your mother is dead, your father is still alive. Your brothers are in there. Sure, we're going to have to work through some things. Sure, it's going to be hard, but they're willing to work on it. They dote on you, Fiona. They follow you. If you choose to forgive your father, I believe they will, too. If you choose not to, I think they'll follow your lead. My point is, you can have a normal life now. The threat of your mother is gone. You told me once that no one cared about you, but now I see a house full of people that would die for you." He ran a hand over her arm. "Myself included. You're free, Fiona. You've got your life back. No, better than that. You've got a brand new one. A clean slate."

"I'm free," she said, feeling the words wash over her. She looked up to the sky, recalling her first moment of freedom with Fletcher, and let out a scream, as loud and carefree as possible. She stood up, arms up in the air, screaming and releasing and crying all at once. For the first time in her entire life, she actually felt freedom. She could taste it. The burdens she'd carried for so long were feeling lighter.

The front door opened, and a worried looking Fletcher and Gunner rushed out, followed by Vaida, Reagan, Jesse, Quinn, and Nora. From the driveway, Nova and Rick hurried their way. Fiona looked at them, meeting Fletcher's eyes and he seemed to understand. "We're free," he whispered, nodding his head.

"We're free," she repeated, a smile on her face so wide it hurt. Fletcher walked toward her, holding out his hand and taking hers. He looked to the sky, screaming in unison with her as they cast away all the secrets and darkness from their past.

It would be there tomorrow, Fiona knew, but for now she could enjoy the peace. She was surrounded by her family, some she'd have to work to earn their trust again, and some who'd have to work to earn hers. But that would come with time. And for the first time, she actually felt like that was something she might have.

She was free. And with freedom, someday happiness might follow. Today, that was enough.

THIRTY-NINE

ONE YEAR LATER

To my daughter,

Nothing about this life has been easy for me. Nothing about any of this has been easy. And then, your father came along. And he is beautiful. And kind. He believes that there is goodness in the world. He sees it even when I can not.

A year ago today, I would've never believed my life could be where it is. I would've never believed I could be expecting you. I don't want you to have to know about all of the darkness I've experienced. I don't want you to know that evil like I've seen even exists. That's why your father is here. To show you the good when I can't find the strength.

I didn't know my father growing up, though he'll be your grandfather now. He is better. Stronger than he was when I needed him the most. But, over time, I've learned to forgive, as others have forgiven me. That's important, my sweet girl, and a lesson I learned very late in life. Forgiveness, even when they don't deserve it, is the only thing that will allow you to forget your burdens.

Your uncles, Gunner, Fletcher, and Jesse, and aunts, Reagan, Vaida, and Quinn, are going to be here for you when I can't. They'll take care of you and make you laugh and help you get away with things I wouldn't. That's okay. It's what your father and I have done for their children.

Speaking of their children, you have a lot of cousins waiting to meet you...Nora and Duncan, Emalee and Skyler, and your new cousin Ryen. Your aunt Vaida will be having her any day. I'm so excited to see you grow up with friends. I want to watch you run through the fields between our houses and laugh with the people who love you. I want to watch you live a full life. I want that more than anything else, my sweet girl.

Our family is complicated. We're messy. I'm learning to accept the mess. I have my blood siblings, Gunner and Fletcher and Quinn—who was sort of a surprise—but I also have a whole extended family that fits into our puzzle pretty perfectly. Holidays are going to be crazy and loud and very expensive.

When I grew up, holidays didn't matter. Nothing really mattered. It was a life I wouldn't wish on anyone, but certainly not you.

You. My little miracle. My angel. The future I never thought that I would have. But I can feel you moving inside of me right now, proof that the future is bright and there is a reason to keep going.

Some days I have to fake it. Some days the strength just isn't there. The strength I see in everyone around me. Your aunt Reagan, who has chosen to put our past behind us. Your uncle Fletcher who, despite everything, has always had more positivity than should be humanly possible. Your aunt Vaida, who has lived through more than any one person should have to, and survived it. Your grandfather, who overcame addiction despite having very little reason to fight it. Your uncle Gunner, who has made a choice to forgive when forgiveness never came easy to him. I see their strength and I want so badly to find it in myself, but I can't. It's just not there.

Some days I hope you'll be my strength, little one. You've given me so much hope already. But some days, I worry you'll just be a piece of me that I can leave behind for your father.

That brings me to the part of this letter I have been dreading writing, but each day as I grow bigger and you become even more real, it's become more obvious that I need to write this.

I hope you never have to see this letter, but I have to be prepared. Like I said, life hasn't come easy to me, so I have to prepare for the worst. No, the almost-worst. The worst thing would be to ever hurt you like I was hurt. I won't let that happen.

The almost-worst, and the purpose of this letter, is that if I lose my strength, if I find myself slipping like my mother did, I will have to leave you. And this letter is all that you'll have of me.

So, I'm writing this letter to give you all the motherly advice I hope to give you in person.

1. *Never let another person lay their hands on you. You can say no. You should say no. You always have a choice.*

2. *Don't look for love in others when you need to find it in yourself.*
3. *Don't you dare settle for good enough. Great is coming.*
4. *When you need help, ask. You don't have to do this alone. You will never be alone.*
5. *Live. Live this complicated, messy, beautiful life. Live it as much as you can. Take every opportunity you get. Learn to say yes more than no. Understand that life can, and does, end in the blink of an eye.*
6. *Forgive. Forgive those that hurt you and move on. You don't have to forget it. In fact, you probably shouldn't forget it. Hurt makes you stronger.*
7. *The last, and probably most important thing, don't ever doubt how much you are loved. Because you are. Even if I'm not here to tell you. Even if one day, you find yourself alone. Know that you were brought into this world surrounded by people who love you. And know that no matter what, your life is one that will move mountains.*

I love you.
Forever hoping you will be stronger than me,
Your mommy,
Fiona

FROM THE AUTHOR

Dear Reader,

Thank you for reading the final book in The Messes Series. I genuinely hope you have enjoyed each and every one of these stories and have fallen in love with these characters like I have.

This series started with one book—one love story. The Cleaner was supposed to be all we'd ever hear about The James family. But, when it was finished, I received so many amazing messages, emails, and reviews begging for more. And guess what? *I wanted more, too.*

So, here we are. Six months and three books later. And I can't thank you enough. These characters and their stories have absolutely changed my life. They've helped to grow my career: placing me on two separate bestsellers lists, introducing me to new fans all over the world, and helping me to reach multiple milestones I once thought would be years away. But, more than that, they helped me to grow. I laughed with them, cried with them, got mad at them, got revenge with them, and most importantly…fell in love with them.

If you have enjoyed this series, I humbly ask that you consider leaving a review on the site where you purchased this copy and anywhere else books can be reviewed. Reviews are so important to authors and I can't tell you how much I would appreciate it.

If you are interested in learning more about my future work, please consider joining my mailing list. I keep my readers up to date with important info and nothing else. I promise there will be no spam and you can unsubscribe at any time. Interested? Just visit kierstenmodglinauthor.com

If you read my note at the beginning of the book, I mentioned four "Easter eggs" (surprise characters from other books)…did you catch them? If so, I would love to hear from you! Feel free to contact me via my website or Facebook.

Again, a huge thanks for reading!

Stay Messy!

XO,

Kiersten Modglin

ACKNOWLEDGMENTS

This book was so hard for me to write. Not only was it a traumatic story, but it was also the end of a series that will stay with me forever.

As I prepared to type 'The End', I began to think about all of the amazing people that contributed not only to this book but to the series as a whole.

Just like Fiona couldn't be alone forever, I could never do this alone. And so, to the following people, I am eternally grateful:

To *my amazing husband*: thank you for all you do for our family. Thank you for making me fall more in love with you every day and for giving my swoony characters a run for their money.

To *my family*: thank you for believing in me from day one and never letting me give up.

To *my PA, Brittany*: thank you for being my "book person". I don't know what I'd do without you. You make this entire, lonely journey feel a little less lonely.

To *my Twisted Readers, Street Team, and Review Team*: thank you for being my cheerleaders, for keeping my corner cozy, and for being the only reason I keep typing some days. You guys keep me going and I don't know what I'd do without you.

To *my betas*, Brittany, Kim, and Janise: thank you for peeling back the mess (pun intended) of my books and helping me find the gold!

To *Rachel Renee, Debi Schmieks, and Sherry Sias*, readers who won a chance to make an appearance in this story: I hope you enjoyed your characters! I had so much fun bringing them to life. Though they were all questionable at best (haha!), they were so important to the story and to the strength Fiona was forced to find.

To *my editor*, Sarah West from Three Owls Editing: you are amazing! Thank you for helping me to make sure I am putting out the best product possible. Your tips, insights, and opinions mean so much to me. I couldn't do this without you!

To *my PR Team at IndieSage*: thank you for working tirelessly to get my books in front of new readers. You guys are the best!

And last, but most importantly, to *you*: thank you for reading this story. Thank you for supporting my dream. I truly believe I have the best fans out there. I appreciate every email, every review, every purchase, and every single person who tells someone new about my work. You are the reason I am able to get up every day and do what I love most—write. And for that, I can never thank you enough.

From the bottom of my heart, I hope this story, this series, has meant something to you. I hope you'll remember these characters for years to come. We've laughed with them and cried with them and they've taught us so many lessons. They are a mess, but they are, and always will be, our mess.

XO,

Kiersten Modglin

ABOUT THE AUTHOR

KIERSTEN MODGLIN is an Amazon Top 10 bestselling author of psychological thrillers and a member of International Thriller Writers, Novelists, Inc., and the Alliance of Independent Authors. Kiersten is a KDP Select All-Star and a recipient of *ThrillerFix*'s Best Psychological Thriller Award, *Suspense Magazine*'s Best Book of 2021 Award, a 2022 Silver Falchion for Best Suspense, and a 2022 Silver Falchion for Best Overall Book of 2021. She grew up in rural western Kentucky and later relocated to Nashville, Tennessee, where she now lives with her husband, daughter, and their two Boston terriers: Cedric and Georgie. Kiersten's work is currently being translated into multiple languages and readers across the world refer to her as 'The Queen of Twists.' A Netflix addict, Shonda Rhimes superfan, psychology fanatic, and *indoor* enthusiast, Kiersten enjoys rainy days spent with her nose in a book.

Sign up for Kiersten's newsletter here:
kierstenmodglinauthor.com/nlsignup

Sign up for text alerts from Kiersten here:
kierstenmodglinauthor.com/textalerts

kierstenmodglinauthor.com
www.facebook.com/kierstenmodglinauthor
www.facebook.com/groups/kmodsquad
www.twitter.com/kmodglinauthor
www.instagram.com/kierstenmodglinauthor
www.tiktok.com/@kierstenmodglinauthor
www.goodreads.com/kierstenmodglinauthor
www.bookbub.com/authors/kiersten-modglin
www.amazon.com/author/kierstenmodglin

ALSO BY KIERSTEN MODGLIN

STANDALONE NOVELS

Becoming Mrs. Abbott

The List

The Missing Piece

Playing Jenna

The Beginning After

The Better Choice

The Good Neighbors

The Lucky Ones

I Said Yes

The Mother-in-Law

The Dream Job

The Nanny's Secret

The Liar's Wife

My Husband's Secret

The Perfect Getaway

The Roommate

The Missing

Just Married

Our Little Secret

Widow Falls

Missing Daughter

The Reunion

Tell Me the Truth

The Dinner Guests

If You're Reading This...

A Quiet Retreat

ARRANGEMENT TRILOGY

The Arrangement (Book 1)

The Amendment (Book 2)

The Atonement (Book 3)

THE MESSES SERIES

The Cleaner (The Messes, #1)

The Healer (The Messes, #2)

The Liar (The Messes, #3)

The Prisoner (The Messes, #4)

NOVELLAS

The Long Route: A Lover's Landing Novella

The Stranger in the Woods: A Crimson Falls Novella

www.ingramcontent.com/pod-product-compliance
Lightning Source LLC
Chambersburg PA
CBHW030608310726
48979CB00003B/617
9781956538380